*Great. Just gre*
*between destro*
*hooking up with ujuj jerk jace.*

With a snarl on her lips, she stepped off the platform, marched straight toward Mr. Blue Eyes, and stopped two feet in front of him.

"What are you doing?" he growled. "You have a show to put on."

"You," she pointed to his face, "will be silent."

He frowned in question.

She reached up and pulled his head to hers, planting a lingering kiss on his lips. To her surprise, it felt kind of good. *Warm, soft, sensual lips.* Very surprising.

She snapped her head back and pointed in his face. "Okay, soft lips, you will meet me at my hotel room after the event."

He cocked one dark brow. "Why would I do that?"

"Because if you do not, I will hunt you down, remove your beautiful smooth olive skin that seems to be well moisturized despite your rough manly exterior, and then I will dismember you, starting with that foul tongue."

# OTHER WORKS BY MIMI JEAN PAMFILOFF

## COMING SOON!
The Librarian's Vampire Assistant
Skinny Pants (Book 3, The Happy Pants Café Series)
Digging A Hole (Book 3, The Ohellno Series)
Check (Part 3, Mr. Rook's Island Series)

## THE ACCIDENTALLY YOURS SERIES
(Paranormal Romance/Humor)
Accidentally in Love with…a God? (Book 1)
Accidentally Married to…a Vampire? (Book 2)
Sun God Seeks…Surrogate? (Book 3)
Accidentally…Evil? (a Novella) (Book 3.5)
Vampires Need Not…Apply? (Book 4)
Accidentally…Cimil? (a Novella) (Book 4.5)
Accidentally…Over? (Series Finale) (Book 5)

## THE FATE BOOK SERIES
(Standalones/New Adult Suspense/Humor)
Fate Book
Fate Book Two

## THE FUGLY SERIES
(Standalones/Contemporary Romance)
fugly
it's a fugly life

## THE HAPPY PANTS SERIES
(Standalones/Romantic Comedy)
The Happy Pants Café (Prequel)
Tailored for Trouble (Book 1)

Leather Pants (Book 2)
Skinny Pants (Book 3) SPRING 2018

## IMMORTAL MATCHMAKERS, INC., SERIES
(Standalones/Paranormal/Humor)
The Immortal Matchmakers (Book 1)
Tommaso (Book 2)
God of Wine (Book 3)

## THE KING SERIES
(Dark Fantasy)
King's (Book 1)
King for a Day (Book 2)
King of Me (Book 3)
Mack (Book 4)
Ten Club (Series Finale, Book 5)

## THE MERMEN TRILOGY
(Dark Fantasy)
Mermen (Book 1)
MerMadmen (Book 2)
MerCiless (Book 3)

## MR. ROOK'S ISLAND SERIES
(Romantic Suspense)
Mr. Rook (Part 1)
Pawn (Part 2)

## THE OHELLNO SERIES
(Standalones/New Adult/Romantic Comedy)
Smart Tass (Book 1)
Oh Henry (Book 2)

# THE
# GODDESS OF...

## (Oh heck! I can't remember.)

### The Immortal Matchmakers, Inc., Series
### Book Four

## MIMI JEAN PAMFILOFF

*A Mimi Boutique Novel*

Cover Design by Earthly Charms (www.earthlycharms.com)
Creative Editing by Latoya C. Smith (lcsliterary.com)
Line Editing and Proof Reading by Pauline Nolet
(www.paulinenolet.com)
Formatting by bbebooksthailand.com

# THE GODDESS
# OF
# FORGETFULNESS

# WARNING

This book contains bad sexy men, offensive language, randy gods, tongue kissing, sex (but not enough, I'm sure), horrible jokes, go-go boots, a missing unicorn, evil mermen, political incorrectness, brutal honesty, and a crazy plot twist only longtime Mimi fans will see coming (maybe).

If you do not like books containing bad sexy men, offensive language, randy gods, tongue kissing, sex (but not enough, I'm sure), horrible jokes, go-go boots, a missing unicorn, evil mermen, political incorrectness, brutal honesty, and a crazy plot twist only longtime Mimi fans will see coming (maybe), then please consider yourself warned.

And then read the book anyway because, really, life is short, and it's just a dang book. What have you got to lose? Think about all of those horrible B movies you've watched on Netflix recently because you've already binged on your favorite shows and there's nothing else to watch. This might be better than those. Or not. But you'll never know unless you try.

As for my awesome fans who've patiently waited for this book…let's get this party started with an F-bomb.

XOXO,
*Mimi*

# CHAPTER ONE

"Gods fucking dammit!" With the loud intro music thundering in her ears and the bright lights beckoning her to the stage, the Goddess of Forgetfulness extended her right hand and cringed at her numbing fingertips. "This can't be good." And she certainly couldn't go out there and perform like this. Because the tingling wasn't some sort of deity carpal tunnel. It was the onset of a much, *much* bigger problem. The godly doomsday sort.

"Bite me, evil Universe. You can't have me!" She shook out her hands, straightened her spine, and stomped the nonexistent dust from her white go-go boots like a Spanish bullfighter summoning courage. Twenty thousand well-deserving mortals from Ibiza, Spain awaited her just on the other side of the black curtain. The town needed her. They needed to laugh and dance and lose themselves in the music. Not that they would die if they didn't, but everyone knew the world thrived on vibes.

*And, honey, there are a whole helluva lot of bad vibes sailing around the planet right now.* It was her divine duty to help turn this earthly crap-cruise of negativity around. *And my humans need to dance.*

She lifted her chin and stepped forward—

"Ooph!" she grunted, unexpectedly colliding with something huge and solid. Suddenly, she was falling, her legs tangled with the other person's.

She landed on her back with a grunt, a very warm body on top of her.

"Get off me!" Forgetty screamed, realizing she was buried beneath a man-shaped mound of muscles wearing an "I heart DJ Whatsherface" T-shirt.

Yes, yes. She was DJ Whatsherface—the world's most anti-famous DJ, known for her addictive, hypnotically sexual spins as much as she was for everyone being unable to remember her. "*Yeah! Let's go see…that lady. She's the best. I think?*" Or, "*I can't remember her name or what she looks like, but I know I really want to see her and forget her again! Woohoo!*"

*It's so weird being me,* she thought quickly, taking notice of the offender's sky-blue eyes, with lavender flecks, boring down on her.

*Wow.* Her breath jammed into her lungs, which stuck in the inflated position.

"Well, well, well…who do we have here?" he said in a deep melodic voice, not the least bit concerned about having knocked her over or being on top of her.

*I will have to vanquish him. But after the show.*

"Remove yourself at once, you pesky mancritter," she snarled, "or I will hit you with something so powerfully vegetative, even your drool will have drool."

Still on top of her, the man slid his arms to her wrists and pinned her down. His crisp blue irises flickered to full-on lavender and then back again.

*Huh? What was that?* It must've been the stage lights.

"Now, now." He chuckled wickedly, seeming perfectly at home nestled between her thighs. "No need to be impolite. It was a simple mistake—of which, I forgive you. Just be more careful where you're walking next time."

Her mouth fell open.

"What? Cat got your tongue?" His smug smile grew. It was then that she noticed the supple fullness of his lips and his short dark beard that matched the brown roots of his long, dirty blond hair.

*Fine. He's hot. But how dare he not fear me and infer that a cat could best me or my tongue? I am a great and powerful deity. Yay me!*

"No, baby," she purred, preparing to blast him with a dose of her powerful light. "But this pussycat does have a bite." *Three, two, on—*

The man jumped off her, getting to his feet and stumbling back. "Gah!" He winced in pain.

*Oopsies,* she thought sadistically. Humans could not tolerate prolonged contact with a deity unless the human wore black jade to blunt the god's energy. If a god—say one with a lot of extra time on her hands—focused her thoughts, she could rile up her cells and get them to release a burst of light. Too much would kill a person. But just the right amount?

"Owww…" The man bent his well-built frame, planting his ripped arms on his knees. He had black geometric shapes tattooed on his muscled forearms. She'd seen those symbols before but couldn't remember where.

*Hmmm. Strange. Not like me to forget things.* It was she who made others forget—their pain, their anger, their shopping lists.

"What the hell was that?" He panted toward his heavy leather boots.

"It's you. Fucking off." A satisfied grin crept over her lips as she sat up, grateful for having worn underwear beneath her short skirt tonight. Normally, she liked to free-cooter it, but it was January.

His head of long silky hair whipped up, and his abnormally handsome face—which she ignored, because…*Ick him!*—displayed a condescending frown.

"Me-fucking-yow, asshole," she added.

He brought himself upright, his powerful pecs stretching out the front of his DJ Whatsherface fan T-shirt. His wide shoulders were the perfect size to support his very solid arms, and he looked to be at least seven feet tall like her brothers—not that the gods were really related. They'd all been birthed from cosmic soup for the Universe's amusement.

"Wrong sound, sweetheart. Try barking." He turned and started walking away, still not bothering to help her up.

*Wait…barking? Barking? I will smite him!*

She hopped to her feet. "Hey! Get back here, buddy. I am nobody's bitch!"

Just before he turned the corner around the black stage curtain, she could swear she saw him chuckling—those broad, strong shoulders shaking.

"What's so funn…" She looked down at her shirt, remembering her outfit—a hot pink miniskirt and a tight white T-shirt that said "BITCH" on the front. On the back, "*Perra Sucia*," or dirty bitch in Spanish.

She crinkled her lips and planted her hands on her sides. The shirt had been funny this morning when she'd put it on, looking for something edgy to wear. Kind of like saying "yeah, I'm a badass" in two languages. Now she just felt stupid.

*Because he ruined it.* She would find him later and set him straight. Right now, she needed to get on with the show.

She closed her eyes, gathering herself. *Get it together, goddess. It's time to party.* She released a soothing breath and opened her heart to the awaiting masses outside. She had a job to do.

*Yes, and now you have two.* Because that numbing in her fingertips could only mean one thing: Her countdown had begun. If she didn't find a man—her man—she would turn evil.

*And gods help us all.* A rogue Forgetty meant an irreversible worldwide amnesia epidemic.

# CHAPTER TWO

"What? Oh, pickles!" Cimil, Goddess of the Underworld, yelled at her sister Forgetty through her pink Bedazzled cell phone while staring at the towering pile of Twinkie boxes in her cart. She hated shopping at club stores, especially in the middle of downtown LA, but sometimes a goddess just needed Twinkies. A lot of freakin' Twinkies.

*And now this? Thank goodness I made it here before the store closed.*

"What do you mean your evil switch has been triggered? You can't flip!" Cimil pushed the shopping cart forward, behind the man buying an obscene amount of whipped cream. She would have to follow him home—clearly the man was up to no good. "Whatsyourface, you know I'm already up to my eyeballs with flippin' flippers. The unmated gods are dropping like flies. Or mom tits. My jugs will never be the same after giving the old boob juice to my quadruplets." Really, nothing on her petite, immortal body would be the same. Even her once silky red hair looked like a tumbleweed. On fire.

Whatsherface's forlorn voice came through the

phone. "Don't play dumb, Cimil. I'm sure you saw this coming, which is why I'm pissed. You could have at least warned me."

No. Cimil had not seen this coming. Just like she hadn't known the Universe would be getting all pissed off at the gods, messing with the unmated immortals—the good were turning evil, evil turning good. Only those with a significant other were safe, as they had someone to prevent their yin from yanging.

*Or yang from yinning?*

"I woulda warned you," said Cimil, "but I was busy not seeing jack because I'm banished! Remember? You all voted to take away my powers, so now sorting out the future is like pouring alphabet soup into my ears. Not so effective—unless it's Monday. Then pour away. Other than that, I'm flying blindfolded, which I sucked at even when I had my powers—no wings!" Listening to the dead, who existed on another plane where time didn't exist, was where she rocked it. The deceased would babble about the future, and she listened for big bad events to come and then helped everyone change course. Only now that her brethren had taken away her powers and sentenced her and her brother Zac, the God of Temptation, to the mortal world until they matched up one hundred immortals (a sad attempt to teach them about love and helping others—*har, har—never gonna happen*), she could no longer decipher the billions of dead voices speaking all at once.

"Whatever, Cimil." Whatsherface sighed. "Doesn't matter now. We're all screwed."

"Yes, but once you lose your nutshells, we won't remember, so who really cares?" The Goddess of Forgetfulness would slide into darkness, unleash her powers, and wipe out the memories of billions of humans, thirteen gods, thousands of vampires, a handful of incubi, a few hundred mermen and mermaids, the demigod army, the were-penguins, and every other evolved species of corporeal beings on the planet.

*Except the sea turtles. They should be safe.* Of course, they weren't really from this planet.

"Cimil! Get that useless head of yours out of your butthole!" Forgetty barked. "This isn't like some Forgetty weekend special where I bump into you and it wears off like a bad hangover. This is catastrophic. Anyone exposed to the full force of my powers won't be getting their memories back. Ever. Humans will forget who they are and how to perform important tasks like reading or growing their own food. Hell, they won't even know how to wipe their asses or brush their teeth. Is that the world you want to go back to? Because we've been there. And it wasn't pretty!"

"Ewww...I see what you mean. I definitely don't want bad breath making a comeback. Bathing is also good. Remember when humans used to slather themselves in lard and scrape it off like nasty

BO butter and—"

"Yes. I remember," Forgetty snapped. "Hygiene is an olfactive blessing."

"Then you'll just have to teach them, because you'll still remember how, right? You can create the Forgetty University of Ass Wiping and Dangly-Bit Washing. It'll be a hit!"

Forgetty groaned. "Cimil, this isn't a joke. And frankly, dirty danglies are the least of our problems. There are humans with babies, elderly parents, and pets. And what about the animals at the zoos? Who will feed them? And what about those who look after nuclear power plants? The reactors will decay if no one maintains them. And it's not like humans will be able to simply pick up a book and relearn everything; they'll all be illiterate. And babbling like naked monkeys."

"Oh! Well, the sea turtles can translate. They speak babble. And we can train Minky to disarm the planet from all sources of radiation. If only I knew how to retire nuclear reactors. And where Minky was." The last time her crazy unicorn had disappeared, she'd been locked up in an Egyptian tomb by a bunch of Roberto's vampires. Roberto, an ex-pharaoh, was now her beloved hubby, but it still chapped her chaps when she thought about how they'd turned Minky into a bloodsucking demon unicorn.

"Cimil, stop cracking jokes and tell me you have a plan," groaned her sister.

"Errrr…I have a plan?" *I really don't. Other than eating Twinkies.*

"I'm serious."

"So am I?" Cimil scratched the side of her mouth.

"Stop it! You have to help me find my mate. Throw me one of those immortal mixer parties like you and Zac did last month."

That party had been for their brother Belch, aka Acan, aka God of Wine and Decapitation—*so fun!*—who was all settled now with a really nice mortal that owned a fitness club. Honestly though, Cimil and Zac couldn't take credit since they hadn't helped with the party for one simple reason.

"Yeah, I meant to tell you. We have a little issue." Cimil began tapping her candy apple red nails on the metal handle of the cart, impatiently waiting for whipped-cream man to unload his cases. "Hurry it up, mister. And don't think I don't know what you're up to." She gave him her 'you've got a date with disembowelment' look, and the man's ruddy face turned ghost white. He began tossing his items onto the belt like he was in a competition for fastest checkout.

"What was that?" Forgetty asked.

"Nothing a little house call won't fix. But as I was saying, Zac has flipped, which I think you're aware of."

"Yes…?" Forgetty groaned with dread.

"And we've been hunting for him, searching

high and low, near and far, wide and narrow, in and out—"

"Cimil! Get on with it."

"What was I saying?" She honestly couldn't remember. The Twinkies had started talking. *Eat us, eat us...*

"You were talking about searching for Zac!" Forgetty yelled in a panic.

"Ah, yes. Our best soldiers have been tracking him—okay, really, they're just following the trail of dead bodies, and we think we've located him. That's the good news."

"What's the bad news?" Forgetty asked.

"He found where I've hidden Tula. Or...he will find Tula, in thirteen minutes and five seconds. And Minky, who was supposed to whisk her away to safety should this event take place, has gone missing." That's right. Disappeared. Right in the middle of an important mission—thus the Twinkies. To boot, Tula was special, her heart made of pure goodness. She could only love, hope, and forgive. It was the reason Tula had been hired to be their assistant at the matchmaking agency she and Zac had set up in order to expedite paying their penance of having to match up one hundred immortals. Tula was supposed to be perfect for Zac since he couldn't tempt her incorruptible heart.

*Or so I'd thought.* Nothing had turned out as planned.

Step #1: Zac was supposed to become obsessed

with Tula. *Check!*

Step #2: After realizing he couldn't tempt her, he was supposed to grow up and rise to the occasion in order to be worthy of her. *Check!*

Step #3? *Super-duper backfire!* Zac had been told repeatedly to stay away from Tula, because he wasn't good enough and would only destroy her. However, instead of bettering himself and then claiming Tula, as it was meant to be, Zac had walked away in order to protect her—his love was just that strong. The result being that he'd flipped to Team Evil.

*Well, fuckity, fuck, fuck-fuck!*

"Jesus. Zac is going to kill Tula," Forgetty muttered. "You have to do something."

"I've warned our friends on the island that he's coming. They'll be ready. They'll capture him."

"Island? Oh no. Cimil, please tell me you didn't."

"What?" she spat. "It was the only place I could think to hide her." And she had sent Minky along for added protection. *Yeah, only now Minky's nowhere to be seen. Or unseen? Whatever.*

"Are you out of your freaking mind, Cimil? That island is the last place you should've sent someone like Tula. Those men will chew her up, spit her out, and make her into a sex slave— willingly, of course."

True. No woman could resist the manly hotness on the island of El Corazón. But we were talking

Tula here. She'd resisted being tempted by Zac—in fact, she'd only begun to have feelings for him *after* he stopped being a selfish prick whose only interest had been seducing her. Once she saw him trying to put her first, resisting his urges to tempt her into his bed, she fell head over granny panties for him. Tula was a very conservative dresser.

"I'm sure she'll be fine," Cimil said. "Just as long as she doesn't disobey her hosts. Or challenge anyone to a swim for control of the island. Besides, I've made it clear they are to protect her at any cost, and they've promised to do so in exchange for my agreeing to never, ever, ever darken their doorstep again." Sad, because she so loved their s'mores night. These dudes knew how to roast a marshmallow, and she was, after all, the Goddess of S'mores. And garage sales, unicorn wrangling, planetary destruction, lying, mayhem, and the underworld. "And I'll have you know that at this very moment, they are preparing for Zac's arrival. It's going to work out fine."

*Maybe.*

*Okay, probably not.*

"And if you're wrong, Cimil? What then?" Forgetty asked.

"I'm never wrong! Except on Tuesdays, Wednesdays, Thursdays—okay! I'm off my game, but this is all your fault for taking away my powers when everyone knows how important I am to keeping the planet safe. Except when I'm creating mayhem and plotting Earth's destruction. But I always save us in the end, don't I?"

Forgetty groaned. "I wish my powers worked on myself, because I'd really liked to forget this entire conversation."

"Me too! Because if I'm wrong again, and Zac gets his hands on Tula, then he will do bad, bad things to her, which will likely end in her death. Good news is that you don't have to worry! We're all screwed anyway because now you're flipping and there is no mate for you. You're destined to be forgotten for eternity. Okay. Gotta go. My turn to pay." Cimil ended the call, feeling like she'd forgotten something, a common symptom when engaging with her sister.

A text suddenly popped onto Cimil's phone.

FORGETTY: *I know you already forgot! So here's the "sitch" in writing: I'm flipping. You need to find me a mate! Yesterday!*

Cimil scratched the side of her head. "But I can't time travel. She must have the wrong number."

☙ ❧

Zac, God of Temptation, prepared the yacht for his date with destiny—aka obtaining total submission from Tula—by dumping the entire crew overboard into the dark ocean. They were dead anyway since he only had need for the captain, who, at present, was locked in the utility closet. *Someone's gotta steer later while I shag the wholesome goodness from my little temptress.*

Zac pushed back his mane of awesome, shiny, badass, black hair and looked out over the railing at the lights of the island hidden from the world—the mortal world. But he was no mortal. He was a fucking evil deity, ready to burn it all to the ground and take what was his: Tula, who'd been taken by Cimil and hidden from him.

Zac grinned, thinking of how much fun he was about to have tonight, killing the men guarding Tula along with everyone on the island—save Tula, of course. No speedy throat-slitting for her. He would take things slow, savoring every moment of breaking her.

*You think you're so above me, don't you? You think you can play games with a god. Well think again, little mortal. When I'm done with you, your heart will be as black as mine.*

Zac shed his black T-shirt and leather pants, preparing to jump overboard and swim ashore, cloaked in the cover of night. He grabbed his hunting knife and checked the edge of the blade. "Perfect for skinning giant fish."

"I think not," said a deep voice behind him.

Zac whipped his naked body around, spotting the shadow of what appeared to be a large naked male with dark camouflage goo on his skin.

*Merman…* Zac growled inside his head. "I had

no idea guppies were nocturnal."

The warrior—equal in size at seven feet with equally large muscles, but not as badass looking or nearly as handsome or evil—flashed his white teeth in a predatory grin. "We are not fish. We are men. Mer-men. And you, Zac, are about to have your ass kicked by one."

Zac threw back his head and laughed into the wintery night sky. "Ahh, good one. And I suppose you think you'll be the one to best me—a cutthroat asshole who doesn't give two fucks—or three or four and so on—about anything."

The merman nodded with a cold stare. "Sounds about right to me."

Zac shrugged. "All right. Don't say I didn't warn you." He began rolling up his invisible sleeves. After all, he was naked, 'cause, really, who gave a fuck? *Or three or four and so on…* "Bring it, Dory."

Suddenly, men covered in the same greasy black goo silently emerged from the water, slithering over the yacht's railing, hunting knives clenched in their bright white smiles.

*I'm surrounded. By obsessive teeth brushers.* "And look. You're all naked, too." Zac snickered with delight. "Because, really, what kind of fight would this be if you weren't willing to put your balls on the line."

"Zac." One merman stepped forward. His size wasn't as substantial as the others, but he had a presence.

"Oh, oh, oh. Lucky-fucky me! The infamous Roen. So we meet at last." Now this was getting good. *King of the mermen and me. Me winning. Me killing his men. Me taking Tula. It's a happy day worthy of a commemorative statue. Or a Netflix special.*

Roen dipped his full head of hair, which appeared to be streaked with the same dark goo covering his naked body and face. "The pleasure is all mine, Zac. Especially if you surrender now because there isn't a chance in hell we'll be letting you anywhere near our mates and children."

Zac bobbed his head slowly, trying to hide his utter giddiness. "I accept that challenge and up the ante. I will kill your men, capture you, and then go after your mates and offspring. Those who do not resist will be captured, and I will then allow you to choose one woman or child to live—'cause I'm generous like that."

Roen shook his head slowly. "Zac, Zac, Zac, we have survived much worse than you. So, as a favor to your bat shit of a sister, Cimil, I will give you one last chance to surrender. But I repeat, you will not be leaving this boat in one piece. You will not lay a hand on any child or female on that island, your Tula included."

"She's mine!" Zac roared. "Mine! I will take her and do as I fucking please."

"Tula wants nothing to do with you." Roen offered a smug grin. "She can't stand the sight of you."

*No. Tula wants me. She's just too pious to admit it.*

Zac's fists trembled. "You lie."

"I am a merman. We never lie. Except on Wednesdays, as Cimil has decreed. Today, my friend, is Monday."

Zac's eyes quickly scanned the men surrounding him. "Awesome. I hear Monday is a great fucking day to die." He lunged at Roen, hunting knife drawn.

# CHAPTER THREE

"Excuuuse me?" Forgetty growled at the young woman on the other end of the phone. "What do you mean, 'Mr. Liath is too busy' to talk to me? I'm the headliner." Forgetty had already decided she wasn't going to perform the last two stops of the global rave tour, and Mr. Liath had to know. Otherwise the mortal masses might turn into an animalistic mob. Sure, none of them knew exactly who they were coming to see, but subconsciously they anticipated her. If she bailed and Mr. Liath didn't have a backup plan, it would result in riots, which would cause even more bad juju around the planet. One person was capable of spreading toxic vibes to thousands in a day. For example, a mother snaps at her kids during breakfast. Kids go to school and snap at classmates, who in turn snap at their siblings, tutors, and parents. Or worse yet, they get into it with the teacher, who then snaps at one hundred kids that day. Bad moods were like a winter cold on an airplane. Very contagious.

"This is urgent. Life-or-death kind of urgent," Forgetty pleaded. "Tell him to make the time and get to the phone right now."

"What was your name again?" the woman asked. "I can't remember."

"Ohhh gods! Bite me." Forgetty ended the call. She would have to go to Monte Carlo to find Mr. Liath, the owner of the tour, before the festivities began tomorrow evening.

Forgetty sat on the king-sized bed of her Airbnb rental and blew out a breath. She wanted to go to Bacalar, Mexico, find the nearest cenote, and swim home one last time before she lost sight of who she truly was—a good goddess. She also missed being in the gods' realm, where she could be a disembodied spirit. No body. And nobody looking at her face and saying, "Hey, don't I know you from somewhere?"

The only reason she'd remained in the human world this long was because of her brother Acan, the God of Wine. He'd needed someone to look after him because he used to be such a troublemaker, always getting wasted, burning buildings down, and getting arrested. She was constantly having to clean up his messes and make humans forget they'd seen him devour entire kegs of beer in one sitting—a supernatural feat to be sure—or that he'd strolled into their establishment drunk and buck naked since he often forgot his pants. Without her help, Acan would've been locked away because the laws governing the gods were very specific; humans were on a need-to-know basis, and any deity who posed a threat to their secrecy posed a threat to them all. The offending god would be stripped of his or her powers and entombed. But Forgetty loved her brother—the only being on the planet who actually remembered her (most of the time) or cared for her—so she'd stayed by his side all these years and kept him out of trouble. Now, he'd found a mate who provided him the balance his soul truly needed. *And great, once I flip, he won't even remember me.* All the gods would go right back to ground zero.

"Fuck. Me." She covered her face and whooshed the air from her lungs. Without warning, her mind shifted to the man from last night with the wicked blue eyes and supremely male body. *So strong.* She had watched him from afar carrying equipment right after her mind-blowing performance of mash-ups that included her favorite '70s tunes, like "Kung Fu Fighting" by Carl Douglas and "Boogie Shoes" by KC and the Sunshine Band; or '80s hits like "Hungry Like a Wolf" by Duran Duran and "Careless Whisper" by George Michaels. The young humans loved her techno mash-ups, likely unaware they were listening to their parents' music. But a goddess as old as her had come to learn that humans were cyclical in their tastes. Everything came back, repackaged with a twist, but there were a few original ideas.

*Okay. The turducken excluded.* Speaking of turkeys, when she found the event owner, she would be sure to mention the hot idiot roadie. Sexy or not, he deserved to be punished.

Forgetty stood from the bed and grabbed her

enormous yellow suitcase, which matched her tank dress and golden hair—because she was cool like that—bidding adieu to the shimmering turquoise waters of Ibiza, Spain, a place filled with warm people, rich history, and relaxing vibes.

"I'm definitely coming back here after I'm cured," she thought aloud, halfway out the door.

*Wait.* She stopped in her tracks. *I won't ever see this place as is again.* Though the Universe might change course and correct the strange path they were all on, the damage left behind after she flipped would be irreversible. Nothing would ever be the same—not the planet, not the people on it, and certainly not this beautiful town or any of the other breathtaking places she'd seen on this tour. She'd been to dozens of pristine beaches all across Europe—the closest thing she'd had to a vacation in fifty thousand years. Now, it all felt like a big farewell tour.

*Godsdammit, there has to be one eligible man on this planet for me to love.* The trick, however, was more complex. He had to love her back, and love— the true, lasting kind—generally required both parties remembering each other.

"Well, it's love at first sight," she muttered to herself.

*Wait! Maybe I've been thinking about this the wrong way.* She propped her yellow suitcase upright and grabbed her cell from her pocket, pulling up the event itineraries.

*Okay. Okay. This is good.* Tomorrow's event in Monte Carlo would have at least twenty thousand people in attendance, half of them male. Following that, the final event in Rio would be even bigger—fifty thousand. What if she got up on stage and asked if any men there felt this "love at first sight" thing she'd heard so much about from humans?

*Hmmm… It might work. But what if bunches of horny men say yes?* How would she tell the real deal apart from the opportunistic males? Honestly, it was a concern. She wasn't even certain that this love-at-first-sight thing existed. Personally, she hadn't paid much attention to the validity of the notion, simply because she'd always had more pressing worries. Plus humans seemed to grow, fall in love, age, and die in the blink of an eye, like a passing season. But, and a big but at that, if a man could love a woman after seeing her for a few moments, then why couldn't he repeat the act and fall in love with her again and again?

*Yes. That's all I need.* One good man, immortal or human, needed to look across the ocean of people and feel genuine love in his heart for her. And then feel it every time he saw her for "the first time" every day for an eternity.

*It will be like my favorite movie,* Fifty First Dates.

*Wait. Hold on. That would make me Adam Sandler.* She crinkled her nose.

*Who am I kidding? I'm screwed.* Because even if a

suitable match was out there, how would she know who he was? She'd never been in love.

"I've never gotten far enough in a relationship for it to happen." Her powers got in the way, not to mention gods had been very limited on dating choices since they weren't usually attracted to other immortal species and they couldn't get down and dirty with mortals until recently. In her "teen" years, ten to twenty thousand years old, she'd had a few dates with a demon or two, but that was no fun. They were all "Me, me, me. Kill, kill, kill. Hold me?"

*Ooph! No, gracias.*

Things finally changed with the Mayans, when a group of power-hungry, bloodthirsty priests discovered black jade. It was a very potent material only found deep underground in the jungles of Southern Mexico. With its many supernatural properties, the Maaskab priests pioneered the manipulation of dark energy, sifting through air, time travel, and mind control. Worse, this stuff could completely immobilize a god if enough was used.

*Ah, but use just a dash?* It blunted a god's energy, which opened the door to physical contact.

*Just in the nick of time.* Another minute longer and the most powerful of her brethren would have lost their shit. They needed love. It was beautiful when she really thought about it. Humans needed gods to keep them out of hot water. Gods needed humans to show them the path to selfless love. Still, she'd resisted, along with many others, and now the Universe was forcing her hand. The gods would either step up and find a mate or there would be total annihilation.

Every divine cell in her goddess body recoiled with fear. She liked her single life. It was simple and free of the romantic heartache she often witnessed in the dating world.

*Come on. What heartache will there be? I'm a goddess. Hot, smart, devoted, and powerful in my own way.* Plenty of men would want her, and she was bound to find one she could connect with.

*I am a sexy goddess. I am a strong woman. I am a sexy goddess. I am a strong…*

Yes. She could do this.

Forgetty headed downstairs to the meet-up with the tour bus to France.

# CHAPTER FOUR

The drive to Monte Carlo went as expected, meaning horrible. Halfway through the trip, Forgetty dozed off and later discovered they were heading in the wrong direction. Because, yes, you guessed it; the driver forgot where they were going, as did the rest of the passengers—a side effect of being in her presence for an extended period of time.

Twelve hours later, with her copiloting, the tour bus pulled up to a fancy-looking, multistory hotel with a stone façade and classic Europe elegance—pillars, circular driveway, and an impressive fountain.

*Gorgeous,* she thought as she walked through the revolving front door. A room here couldn't cost any less than a few thousand per night. And the lobby, with its soaring domed glass ceiling that sparkled with the last rays of sunlight, only confirmed that Mr. Liath had spared no expense for the headlining talent.

*I have to meet the man.* Because he had incredible taste. *Or not.* His team actually took care of all the event itineraries and travel arrangements, which was why she'd never met the man, not even when they'd been working through the contract for this tour. He was like a ghost, though rumor had it he was really just an old, crotchety money-grubber with a knack for investing in music, entertainment, and the arts. It was even said that he didn't like dance music.

*I bet he's never heard me spin.* She could read a crowd, feel their collective energy, and play the perfect song to edge them up the emotional ladder. By song four, everyone was laughing, smiling, and feeling their entire bodies swell with love. That, in turn, gave her a high like no other. Regardless, this Mr. Liath likely only knew enough about her and her fellow DJs to book the best of the best.

*At least he's got good sense going for him.* And hopefully she could find him at the venue because after tonight, she would be too busy to make the final stop on the tour in Rio. *Once I get on that stage and offer myself up to love, I'll be sorting through thousands of males until I find one suitable enough to be my mate.* Unfortunately, finding Mr. Liath wouldn't be so easy. There were four stages, almost a thousand employees—security, concession workers, janitorial staff, roadies, managers, lighting and sound technicians. She would have to get there early.

*Not a problem!* Now that she'd figured out her plan, she couldn't wait to meet her mate. *I've been waiting seventy thousand years, and tonight is the night! I can feel it!*

❧ ❦

Later that evening, Forgetty prepared for her big event by pinning up her golden hair into an elaborately braided twist, something she rarely did because she preferred stylish comfort over appearance, which usually meant braided pigtails. Occasionally, she would weave white ribbons in her blonde hair and paint her face neon so that the black lights made her look like a crazy creature from another planet. The young humans loved it. Tonight, though, instead of her usual tank dress that left her arms free to move about the turntables, she put on a skimpy, one-shouldered, red dress she'd found in the gift shop downstairs.

Forgetty put on her matching red strappy heels and bright red lipstick and then looked in the full-length mirror in the bathroom—a fancy white marble palace too bright for her taste. Her eyes washed up and down her tall, curvy body. "Yep, my outfit definitely screams I'm open to love." She just wished she wasn't sooo tall.

*I'll just have to find a man who likes giraffes.* She leaned forward, puckered her flaming red lips and fixed a smudge of black eyeliner. With the pound of mascara and smoky makeup caked around her turquoise eyes, they nearly glowed, which was exactly what she wanted. Not that she was opposed to mating with a mortal, but if any eligible immortal males were in the audience tonight, they'd surely notice her eyes—a sign of her divinity.

With her outfit all set, she went downstairs and boarded the awaiting shuttle just outside the grand lobby's front door. It was already filled with staff. *Who are all staring and looking confused. Excellent way to start my night.* It was the same story every time she met people she already knew. They'd go quasi-catatonic for several seconds while their brains hiccupped, knowing she looked familiar but unable to place her in their memories.

"What? Haven't you ever seen a goddess? Who DJs? And is dressed like a hooker from the '80s?"

Everyone shook their heads no.

"Ha-ha. You're all a bunch of comedians." She took the last open seat near the front. She probably shouldn't have said that thing about being a goddess, but they'd all forget in a few moments anyway.

The shuttle departed, and within twenty minutes the vehicle was pulling through the back gate of the Louis II Stadium, an enormous outdoor sports arena and home to the beloved Monaco soccer team. Off in the distance she could see the parking lot overflowing.

*Perfect. A full house.* The more people, the better her chances of finding Mr. Right. *I can't wait!* Plus, the French were wild when it came to these events that looked like a Super Bowl halftime party times

four—multiple stages, lights, and dance perfor-
mances. The rave would go until one a.m., with her
being the last DJ. Fireworks would mark the end of
the event.

*Speaking of fireworks, please let me find some of
my very own tonight.*

The shuttle pulled up to the curb in front of the
employee entrance. With an eager bounce in her
step, she exited the shuttle and headed straight to
the security checkpoint tent, where she would show
her pass and—

*Oomph!* Someone rammed her from the right,
knocking her off her spiked red heels. She flew
several feet, landing on her left hip. The sound of
tearing fabric preceded the burn of her skin scraping
across the cement.

"Motherfucker!" She groaned, rolling onto her
back and cupping the shredded skin on her arm,
only to realize the pain on her hip was way worse.

"Jesus, woman," snarled a deep, baritone voice,
"do you have spatial awareness issues?"

Forgetty's eyes darted to the large man hovering
over her, two shockingly blue eyes glaring down.

*Hey, it's that…* "Asshole! *What* is your deal?" He
was the same barbarian roadie from last night.

*Okay, yes.* He was tall and all ripped biceps, and
also wearing really sexy leather pants, but so the hell
what? The same could be said for lots of stagehands
on this tour. There was Mike, the head of security
with his amazing tats, and Waylon, the sound guy

who looked like a Calvin Klein underwear model, especially when he went around shirtless while setting up. *Such. Nice. Abs.* Point was, a perfect male body didn't mean dick if the guy was, well, a giant dick.

*Oh. I bet he has one of those, too.*

"Ohmygod. Are you okay?" A fellow performer, a young redhead who went by the name We-J, knelt down.

Forgetty snapped out of her very odd mental detour and focused on the man sneering down at her, his eyes narrowed to tight little slits to punctuate his abhorrence.

"Asshole?" he huffed. "Isn't that precious coming from someone like you."

Without bothering to help her up or assist with her injuries, he turned his broad back, donning a snug-fitting DJ Whatsherface T-shirt, and headed into the event, sailing through the security checkpoint.

"This is war." She scowled, propping herself up on her one good elbow. And by war, she meant his death. Normally, she would simply ignore males such as him, delighting in the knowledge that he would soon perish and meet Cimil, who would do bad, bad things to him before dragging him off to the place where evil souls went. *But this guy? Oh, no, no, no, señor.* This guy with his perfect-fitting leather pants, worn and soft and hugging his solid ass in just the right way. Oh, this guy was going down.

We-J helped Forgetty to her feet. "I think you need to go to the medic tent. That scrape looks pretty nasty."

Forgetty inspected the road rash on her exposed hip. Physically, she would be fine and heal up within the hour, but the impact of the fall had torn right through the delicate red fabric of her dress.

"I'm good. Which way are the vendors?" Forgetty asked.

"Take a right after the security checkpoint." We-J pointed the way.

Forgetty dipped her head, realizing her elaborate hairdo had come loose. *Another casualty of Mr. McButthead.*

"Thanks." Forgetty hobbled away, chin held high. As soon as she found new clothes and then Mr. Liath, she would hunt down the bulldozer and make him wish he'd never reached puberty. "Because I'm going to grab him by the short hairs and drag him off to the nearest ditch for a good old-fashioned eye plucking."

࿔ ࿔

Three hours later, Forgetty stood at the edge of the main stage, her search for Mr. Liath having resulted in a suspicious amount of shrugs and "I haven't seen hims." It wasn't possible for the owner of this worldwide dance event, attended by one million people when all was said and done, to be so anonymous. Something was going on, but it could wait. Being over seventy thousand years old had taught her that there were few situations that truly qualified as a mystery, urgent, or worthy of divine intervention. Mr. Liath was likely some scabby old mobster who operated in the shadows.

*Whereas I'm a goddess trying to save the world from terminal amnesia.* No, it wasn't fatal to forget how to wipe one's ass, but not knowing where to find water or what qualified as a food was catastrophic. The way she saw it, unless she did this and did it well, humans were doomed.

Forgetty stepped forward on the stage, staring out at the ocean of curious faces illumined by the lights behind her. She'd asked for the intro music to be shut off, the mic turned on, and the camera crew to film her so that everyone within the arena could see her on the big screens positioned above.

Hands shaking, she wiggled the mic from the stand. *Please, Universe, let him be here.* She cleared her throat and looked down at her lame outfit—some black leggings with green pot leaves and a sweatshirt with "DJ Who. Me?" on the front. Hopefully, her mate would see past the exterior. *Yes, your only real worry should be how to handle the herd of men about to trample the stage.*

"He-hello." She spoke into the microphone, her voice reverbing with an earsplitting shriek for the first few seconds. "I'm-I'm DJ Forgetty, which I'm sure you'll all forget in five point five seconds, but…" She looked down at her now bare feet. She'd had no reason to wear the heels after her dress had been ruined.

*Be strong, Getty. You can do this.*

She gulped hard. "So, this is really awkward, but I've never had a relationship or fallen in love. It pains me to admit it. Truly. But I'm afraid to love someone and then look into his eyes and know he doesn't remember me." She shrugged toward the ground. "So, you see, it's pointless to think I could have anything beyond one night with any male. But if there's any man out there who feels something genuine for me, something deep in his heart—love at first sight—well, I think I could be happy with that. It's more than I've ever expected."

Relief washed over her. She'd put herself out there and said her piece.

Slowly, she lifted her gaze back toward the crowd, preparing for what would come next.

*What the fuck?* Like a deer in headlights, the people stared, completely motionless. Not one man, or woman, moved toward the stage.

She tapped the microphone. Yes, it was on. *What's happening?* There didn't seem to be even one measly taker.

"Are you paying attention? Doesn't anyone feel anything?"

Crickets.

Horror washed over her. "Really? Not one of you has anything to say?" For the first time in her existence, she felt tears of self-pity well in her eyes. She covered her face with her hands and pushed out a breath. "Unbelievable." She was a goddess, for crying out loud. Most men prayed for a female like her at one time or another.

*Fucking figures.*

Just then she felt a pair of eyes on her. She turned her head to see Mr. Asshole Roadie staring from the side of the stage, muscled arms crossed over his chest, and a flicker of something strange in his eyes.

She stared, wondering what the hell he was looking at.

Suddenly, he flashed a cocky smile, like her humiliation pleased him, and then dipped his head of thick dark blond hair before turning and walking away.

Her humiliation turned to anger. "Laugh all you like, buddy," she called out. "Your days are numbered!"

Forgetty swiveled toward the salvation of her turntables. "Let's get this party started," she grumbled and flipped the power switch on her control board. The lights flickered and the masses roared as her techno mash-up of "YMCA" (by The Village People) and "Millennium" (by Robbie Williams) pounded through the speakers.

# CHAPTER FIVE

"No. Please stop!" screamed the naked little man tied to his kitchen table. "I promise I wasn't going to do anything bad—I'm a caterer!"

Cimil replaced the duct tape over his mouth and tugged the knot around his wrist. Yesterday evening, she'd followed the man home from the club store and spied through his window. She hadn't caught him doing anything shady; however, no one bought that much whipped cream unless they were insane—like her—or planning a wrestling match.

*Oh. I wonder if he'll invite me!*

"No more lies!" Cimil yelled. "Today is not Wednesday, and I am a busy goddess. Where do you have the wrestlers hidden? And why was I not invited to the obligatory whipped-cream-licking session that will follow?"

The man's brown eyes widened in terror. "*Mumble, mumble, mumble.*"

"What? Can't hear you." Cimil ripped the tape from his face.

"Ow!"

"You ain't seen 'ow' yet, buddy."

"Please, lady. I don't know who you are or

which hospital you've escaped from, but I'm telling the truth. Check the freezer in my garage. I'm catering a fundraiser for the fire department—"

Cimil's cell vibrated in her shiny pink fanny sack.

"Hold that thought," she said, digging out her phone, thinking it might be her vampire king hubby, Roberto, who was at the zoo with their four tiny antichrists of mayhem—*my prides and joys.*

The caller ID showed a big question mark. Not Roberto. "Whatsyourface? That you?"

"Cimil, I need your help," Forgetty blubbered on the other end of the phone. "You have to throw that immortal singles mixer for me. Fast. My plan failed."

"Sorry. I'm a little tied up at the moment—or shall I say, *tying* up at the moment. Which is really a sad attempt to distract myself because I've yet to hear back from our mer-licious warriors regarding the outcome of their attempt to capture our brother Zac."

"Cimil, this is serious. I just got rejected by ten thousand men. And probably a few hundred women, too."

"Have you considered covering yourself in whipped cream and asking them to lick it off you? I've just come into a large supply of the stuff, so I could help you out."

"What? No. Why would you say that?"

"Say what?" She honestly couldn't remember. In

fact, why was she in this house? *Why is that man tied to a table?* Cimil looked at the phone in her hand. "Who am I speaking to?"

"Dammit, Cimil! Focus. It's me, Getty!"

"Hmmm…sounds vaguely familiar."

"Just stop. Okay? I'm really trying here. I need to find my mate. Can you help me or not?"

"Not."

"So that's it. You're just letting the ship sink, and you won't even lift a finger to help your own sister or the humans in our care."

"Oh, it's Forgetty! Why didn't you just say so? And nope. It is as I've told you. There is no mate for you. You are destined for eternal misery and spinsterhood. Seriously, don't even hope." Honestly, though, who the hell knew? Without powers, Cimil's ability to clearly hear all of the things the dead were saying was impossible, and she only knew of one man in the entire universe who was totally ape shit for Forgetty.

*But that guy is eviiiil.* His soul was so dark that shadows feared him. This dude was so scary that the boogie man dressed up like him for Halloween. *He's so bloodthirsty that even vampires feel like complete pussies in his presence. All right, except for my pharaoh, Roberto, who only feels like a pussy on Saturdays when I dress him like a Sasquatch, which really looks like a big hairy vajay-jay. Hey, why the hell am I talking about this? Is anyone listening? Anyone? Testing, testing.*

No one replied.

"Sorry, Forgetty. Looks like you're on your own," Cimil said.

"Cimil," Forgetty growled over the phone, "I think you're forgetting that once I flip, that's it. Humankind, the gods, everyone with consciousness is toast. Can't you even try to help me? And if not for me, for the sake of the sea turtles?"

"Dammit! That's low, Forgetty. You know I have a hard spot for them—get it, hard spot. Because they have shells and...oh, nevertheturtles mind. Fine. I will take time out of my busy schedule, even though Minky is still missing and Zac is on the loose, terrorizing the masses. But it will be a round of speed dating, and no more." This really was a waste of time; however, Forgetty had always been there for her, though she couldn't recall for what exactly. Or when.

"Great. How much time do you need?" Forgetty asked in a hurried voice.

"A week."

"One week? Can't you do it faster?"

"I've got no assistant, and Zac is off playing serial killer, so I'll have to get to the office and sort through our database of eligible immortal men all on my own. Plus, I need to get your profile up on all of the big dating sites Match.com, Vampirefreaks, clowndating, and fetlife."

"I need a mate, not a night of juggling, fetishes, and fangs."

"Sounds hot to me! But now you're complaining? Really, there is no pleasing you." Someone in her position had to be open to the possibility of finding love anywhere. For example, she'd found her hubby, Roberto, next to a pyramid in Egypt. Then he took her prisoner and turned into a vampire and he stole her unicorn—your typical love story—but it just proved that love could show up in the unlikeliest of places with the least likely people.

"Sorry. Thank you for helping me," Forgetty grumbled.

"Don't mention it. Now have fun in Rio. And don't wear heels next time."

"Hey, how'd you know about—"

"Oops. My other line is buzzing. Gotta go." Cimil switched to the incoming call and went to the fridge to grab a can of whipped cream. "Cimil, Goddess of crispy, deep-fried treats and other evil sundries." She turned and began to cover the naked man on the table with big white dollops.

"Cimil, it is I, Roen," said a dark voice.

Cimil dropped the can on the floor. *Oh god—I mean me—oh me, he doesn't sound happy.* "What's the status?"

"We have Zac."

"Yippy!" Cimil jumped up and down.

"But it has cost us many men, and as such, he will be put down."

Should she tell Roen that gods couldn't die? *Nah…let him figure that one out on his own.*

Roen added, "And by 'put down,' I mean he will be placed in an airtight steel barrel. We will fill it with cement and drop him to the deepest part of the ocean—as our laws dictate. All right, really it is a punishment we made up for you, just in case you show up to our island again. Nevertheless, it seems befitting for Zac, too."

*Jeepers.* Sitting at the bottom of the ocean for all eternity, unable to die, was way worse than…well, dying. It meant that Zac would remain trapped for all eternity. Not even she could rescue him.

*Aquaman could. He can do anything.* She mentally swooned. *Momoa…*

"What would you like us to do with your human, Tula?" Roen asked.

"Why should I care?"

"Uhhh, because you said she was of extreme value to mankind and we were to keep her safe at all costs, which we did. Five good mermen lost their lives."

"And we appreciate the sacrifice, but the situation has changed. Zac and his foibles will be erased from our memories in about eight days. Oh, and I suggest you draw yourselves some pictures on the fine art of butt wiping. It will come in handy. Tootles."

"Cimil! You bat-shit crazy piece of shi—"

Cimil disconnected the call and shrugged. "I don't get why everyone's always so surprised when I throw curveballs. It's my brand." She looked at the trembling man stretched across the table, a few strategic mounds of whipped cream covering his nipples. "Okay, Scooter, let's get this torture session started. Shall we begin with you licking your own nut sack?"

His mouth fell open in terror, but he didn't scream.

Her smile stretched from ear to ear. "Damn, I love my job."

 ҈ ҉

Zac woke to a horrible pain in his chest and a throbbing ache in his skull, quickly realizing the warm wetness between his back and the cement floor wasn't water.

*Fuuuuck.* That had been one hell of a battle, but clearly they'd bested him, and now he was leaking blood.

"Ah, you're awake. About fucking time," said a deep voice.

Zac's eyes strained to see the clean face on the other side of the bars. Roen, king of the mermen. Behind him stood two large warriors. Zac believed one to be Lyle, Roen's brother.

"Hey, pollywogs," grumbled Zac. "Looks like you all had baths. I assume bubbles were involved since you're all a bunch of froufrou pussies?"

Roen sighed with exasperation. "Insult me all you like, God of Limp Dicks, but you're our prisoner, and soon you will be punished for your crimes against my people and the innocent humans you've slaughtered."

Zac slowly brought himself upright, placing his hand on the back of his wet, blood-caked hair. The wound felt closed, which was a pity because clearly he would live, and dying meant freedom. If a deity's body got destroyed, their soul was released from this world. Then they could choose to go to their plane or return to this world through one of their portals, which were really cenotes, or freshwater springs, in the Yucatan jungles of Mexico. *It was all very cool and godly. Unlike mermen.*

"Dream all you like, tuna melt," Zac grumbled. "My brethren will never allow you, a lowly une-volved creature, to do squat to me." *They'll be coming for me to exact their own justice.* Of course, it would be entombment, but only until all was set right with the Universe again. Then he'd be free— bored, awesome, and likely sentenced to a thousand years of matchmaking. *Lame. But whatever.*

"You are mistaken," Roen said with a smirk. "Your brethren do not appear to be the least bit concerned. In fact, Cimil indicated they plan to forget all about you. And ass wiping. I am unsure; the conversation was very confusing."

"No one's forgetting about me. Those pussies can't live without my temptation. I'm the spice of their pathetic eternal lives."

"Nope. I'm pretty sure she said you would be

completely forgotten in eight days."

Zac frowned, his foggy mind picking up on the true meaning. "Did Cimil happen to also mention if my sister, the Goddess of Forgetfulness, would be following in my evil footsteps in these next eight days?"

Suddenly, his holy scaliness—*fine, all right. He isn't scaly. He has very nice tanned skin*—his holy mer-ness seemed uncomfortable. "What do you mean?"

"Let me out, and I'll tell you."

Roen narrowed his green eyes. "I think not."

"Suit yourself."

"Oh, I will. And it suits me to carry out your punishment at sunrise."

"Whatevs." Like he cared. He was evil. And the sooner they carried out their silly punishment, the better.

*Oh, I hope they behead me,* Zac thought. Anything fast would be good. Then he would return to this world and continue his quest to conquer, corrupt, fuck, and possess Tula.

If she resisted, he'd kill her.

Zac saluted Roen. "Aye-aye, catfish."

Roen shook his head. "I cannot begin to articulate how good it will feel to rid the world of you." He turned and left, heading for a set of cement stairs leading up to ground level, his two soldiers on his heels.

Zac suddenly felt cold—in his heart, his mind,

and every space between the molecules of his now bitter soul. *Wait a second. Forgetty is turning. Fuck. Fuck no.* That meant he would forget Tula. The tiniest corner of his heart, still possessing a handful of cells filled with light and goodness, began protesting violently. He could handle anything, do anything, become anything, but losing all memories of her for eternity?

Terror filled him.

*No. This is good,* his evil side argued. *I will finally be free of her.* He lowered himself back down to the sticky blood-soaked floor and smiled up at the gray ceiling. It would indeed be a blessing to be free of his feelings for her. *Think of all the damage I could do to the rest of the world. Best. Evil. Vacation. Ever.*

He catapulted upright. "Who am I joking? My evilness belongs to her." She was the reason he'd flipped. He'd fallen in love with her, but resisted his feelings because Cimil swore he would destroy Tula if he took her as a mate. He simply wasn't good enough for her. But honestly, who was? Tula had the purest, most beautiful aura he'd ever seen on a human.

*Wait. Perhaps I didn't think through my plan very well.* Without a mate, the plague had gotten him anyway. *And here we are.*

Zac pinched the bridge of his nose, unable to think straight. It felt as though someone had shoved rotting cotton candy inside his mind.

*No. You're thinking just fine.* Yes, yes. He knew

what to do. He wanted to dedicate his energies to Tula. He would allow these idiots to do what they pleased, enacting their ridiculous punishment, and then he'd continue as planned. Tula would submit to him or die a torturous slow death. *I will make her pay for her hold over me. I will make her suffer for her goodness.* Humans were not allowed to be better than the gods. It was unnatural.

"Zac! Zac! Ohmygod, are you down there?" a sweet voice called out from the stairwell.

"Tula?"

"Oh my stars!" She quickly shuffled down the stairs, their eyes meeting from across the cold cement room. "What have they done to you?"

Zac's wickedness snickered on the inside, but he put on his lost puppy-dog face. "Tula, I came searching for you, and they beat me."

Her wide blue eyes filled with sadness. "Those barbarians. They said you were crazy and here to hurt me."

*They're right.*

He slowly got to his feet and gripped the steel bars of the cell, offering his sincerest of expressions. "I would never hurt you, my sweet mortal. This is one of Cimil's crazy plots—I think she's turned completely evil. I came because a woman as beautiful as you is not safe with these savages."

Tula, wearing a thin blue flowery dress covering her from neck to ankles—*so sexy! Look at all that prim and properness! I bet she's wearing giant panties, too!*—brushed her hand over her long blonde hair. "I look like a mess. They loaned me a few things, but the women here don't wear much clothing, and the bathroom scares me. I could swear I hear voices every time I turn on the tap water."

*Oh, is Crazy Dirt back?* She was an evil water spirit of sorts that once enslaved the mermen. Nobody knew where she'd gone, but that was a worry for another time.

"You look like a thousand sunsets and a million budding roses to me, Tula," he said. "You could be completely nude, and I'd still want you."

She flashed a demure smile. "I've missed you, Mr. Zac. You and your weird jokes."

That hadn't been a joke. He was the God of Temptation. The fewer inhibitions, the less his interest in a woman.

Tula came up to the bars, placing her soft little hands over his. "I'm going to get you out of there, Zac. I won't let them entomb you at the bottom of the ocean."

"What's this?"

"They plan to put you in an airtight container and sink you so you can't ever be rescued."

*Oh. Not good.*

"But I know where the key to your cell is. You wait here." She turned, heading for the stairs.

*Sweetheart, I ain't going anywhere.* "When will you return?"

"Soon, Zac. Soon. Be ready to run."

*Oh, I'll be ready. Ready to finally crush your snow white soul and make you mine.* But somewhere deep in his heart, he already knew what would happen. Tula's soul was incorruptible. It was why he'd been drawn to her from the first moment they'd met. *She will never give in to me. She is too good.* An image of him wrapping his strong hands around her sweet, pale neck, strangling the life out of her, flooded his mind. *Then she shall die. A punishment for her perfection.*

"Hurry back, my love!" he called out.

# CHAPTER SIX

*I will not scream in hysterics. I will not scream in hysterics. I will not—okay, I'm going to scream in hysterics.* Forgetty white-knuckled the armrests of her seat toward the back of the plane bound for Rio, wondering why she'd gotten on the stupid aircraft to begin with. It always ended the same. Always. But this time, she'd worn a necklace made entirely of black jade, a material used to dampen a god's energy. Her brethren employed it all the time with their human mates, who couldn't survive prolonged physical contact without it. *I was sure this would work!* But no.

The plane banked left again, tilting everyone on their sides and triggering a plane full of whimpers and gasps.

*Dammit.* Perhaps her situation was far worse than she'd thought. With her soul struggling to remain in the light, her energy was likely amped up, almost like when a human had an infection and the immune system went into overdrive.

*Ugh. I really should just get my pilot's license.* Nervously, she glanced out the tiny oval window and slid her cell phone from her pocket to call the only being on the planet who ever truly remembered her, Acan, the God of Wine. He also went by Belch, Dr. Decapitation (a new gift he'd discovered) and Mr. Balls Out. Really, the gods had so many names, one or more for each culture, that they couldn't remember them all. She was the exception. *No name. Not one.* What was the point? No one would remember it.

"Forgetty-getty-wetty!" yelled a deep voice through her phone. "Dear gods, woman! Where the fuck have you been hiding?"

*Or perhaps I've never adopted a name because it will only result in being called things such as "Forgetty Wetty."* No, not because she wet herself, but because whenever her brother talked her into a chugging contest, it inevitably ended with her losing. No one could beat the God of Wine at drinking. He would then poke fun and claim she looked like she might cry. *"Forgetty Wetty lost again!"*

"Do not call me that, brother, or I shall call you the Tighty Whity Mighty." Before he'd found his mate, Margarita, Acan spent his days so drunk that he often forgot to wear pants.

"I cannot claim to feel insulted by that nickname, sister. I am, after all, the party god, and nothing says fun like a fine pair of men's cotton briefs. However, your absence from my New Year's nuptial ceremony and from our joint business ventures is another sour cocktail."

She and Acan owned a worldwide chain of bars

and nightclubs, which they ran together, though she did most of the work since he used to be so unreliable. But now he was all grown up and capable of running things on his own. She deserved this break. Unfortunately, she'd missed his wedding a few weeks ago on New Year's Eve.

"I'm sorry for that." She pinched the bridge of her nose. "And I promise there's a perfectly good explanation—one you know I'm good for. However…"

"Yes?" he pushed.

"Well, I'm currently on my way to Rio and—"

"Dear gods, Getty! Please tell me you are not flying again."

She winced. "Yes. But I wore black jade this time. Only, it doesn't seem to be working."

"Not good, Getty. Not at all." He tsked.

"Well, I'm sorry. How else was I to get to Rio, huh?"

"Why must you go at all?" he barked. "You know what happened the last time you were on an aircraft—and the previous thirty times before that."

The crew and passengers experienced temporary amnesia due to the prolonged exposure to her energy.

"Yes, of course I know. But…" She sighed, wanting with everything in her heart to tell him the really-really. But he really, really didn't need this breed of heartache in his life. For the first time in seventy thousand years, he was happy. He had

Margarita and Jessica, her teenaged daughter. The three of them had become a family, and now was his time to simply live. If she told him she was in trouble and soon the world would fall in to a mental pit of darkness, he'd only panic and try to step in. But what could he do? She would either meet Mr. Mate or she wouldn't. Acan could do little to alter her destiny.

"But what?" Acan prodded.

"Let's table the lecture for the moment. I'm on a plane and need you to guide the pilot through the landing before we run out of fuel."

Acan grumbled on the other end of the line. "Of course, sister. Put the pilot on the phone."

She reached for the call button, and the attendant, a young brunette, showed up immediately.

"Hi. This call is for the pilot." Forgetty held out her phone.

"Sorry, ma'am?"

"Look. I don't have time for this and neither do you. We're about to fall out of the sky, so I suggest you pass this call to the pilot."

The woman's face contorted.

"Bejeezus! Lady," Forgetty barked, "even you must've noticed we've circled the runway eleven times."

"Well," the attendant rubbed her forehead, "now that you mention it…"

"Good." Forgetty wiggled the phone at her. "Take it to the cockpit before we all end up on the evening news."

The woman snatched the device and scurried off.

"Good human."

After a few minutes, Forgetty felt the plane banking to the right, descending quickly.

She leaned back in her seat and whooshed out a breath. "Thank gods Acan knows how to land a 747."

One disaster averted. One to go. This was her last chance to find a mate, meaning she would take the stage one more time. If this didn't work, the fate of the world would be left up to speed dating à la Cimil. No high hopes there.

❧ ❦

Once again Forgetty was amazed by the hotel chosen for her and the other DJs by the event team. Yes, each stop on the tour made a crap load of money, but this time they'd put her up in a penthouse suite of the Belmond Copacabana Palace, a five-star hotel overlooking the ocean. *Another amazing place that won't ever be the same again, unless I find a mate.* She suddenly looked forward to returning to LA one last time, to see their flagship nightclub, the Randy Unicorn, filled with happy customers. Hopefully, she'd make it there before time ran out.

That evening, she took a bubble bath in the

huge tub while she waited for room service—two orders of chocolate chip cookies, a pitcher of caipirinha—the national drink, which tasted sort of like a mojito—and a grilled cheese. *'Cause hey, why not? When you're a goddess, you don't have to worry about weight, health, or your liver getting old.*

After her bath, she curled up on the plush khaki couch, her warm, relaxed body wrapped in the softest guest robe ever, and she flipped through the channels. Most everything was in Portuguese, which was hunky-dory with her. The only language she couldn't get cozy with was Ancient Greek. *Bad memories.* It was a time in her life when all her brethren were getting a day of the year named after them and temples built in their honor. Humans told stories about each of them and made offerings of fruit.

*I got nothin'.* She had never felt so invisible and useless as during that era. *Thank gods that whole obscure-deity-worshipping thing is over.* Humans had mostly forgotten about the gods, so now they were all on the same unglamorous boat. Okay, India being the exception. *All right, and China and Japan and…*

"Oh, bollocks," she grumbled under her breath and flipped to a soap opera before grabbing her plate of gooey grilled cheese. "Yum…" Her eyes rolled inside her head. After today's almost epic tragedy, this was exactly what she'd needed.

A loud knock jolted her from her cheesy Zen

moment.

She looked over her shoulder at the door, thinking the room service people must've forgotten something—not so unusual in her world. Most take-out orders resulted in getting nothing or half of the order correct. *Pepperoni pizza? No. You get cheese, lady. You want lo mein with veggies and pork? How about egg rolls.* She'd become accustomed to getting whatever and making do. Only tonight, the staff had brought her everything she'd requested.

She got up, went to the door, and peeked through the tiny hole. A bellhop stood there with a giant bouquet of red roses and a clear vase.

*Odd.*

She jerked open the door. "Yes?"

"Uh, these are for you." He held them out. "I think."

With hesitation, she reached for them. "Who are they from?"

"Dunno."

"Oh, let me guess. You forgot." Why did she bother to ask?

"They were left at the front desk with your room number." He looked up toward the ceiling. "Where am I?"

*Ugh.* "You're leaving." With flowers in hand, she closed the door. The man would be fine in a few seconds.

She gave one of the buds a whiff, inhaling the sweet tangy scent of the flowers. It had been ages since she'd had roses and that was only because she'd bought them for herself. *No wait. Those were forget-me-nots*—her favorites.

She peeked inside the bouquet to find a tiny card nestled among the leaves. She set the flowers down on the little table next to the couch and opened it. Inside, it simply said *Sorry.*

"Sorry?" *What the hell? Sorry for what?* Then it dawned on her. "Ah. Acan must've sent them." He wanted to cheer her up after her horrible flight. His new mate, Margarita, truly was having a positive effect.

With that, Forgetty settled in for the night in the luxurious king-sized bed. She didn't need to sleep, but like eating, she found the activity enjoyable. She liked shutting down her mind and allowing it to wander the cosmos for a few hours, almost the same sensation as when she was back in her realm. Free to go anywhere, see anything—just exist.

She closed her eyes, drifting off into a dream about lying on a beach of white sand, the warm sun on her face and the gentle breeze floating off the ocean. She could practically taste the salt in the air and hear the waves swishing.

Suddenly, the warmth went away, and when she looked up, a tall, dark figure stood before her, blocking the sun.

Her skin turned ice cold. Her heart stopped beating. The man had no face, no body—he was just a shell of darkness.

"Who are you?" she asked, feeling frightened.

He didn't respond.

"Who?" she yelled.

His hand stretched out, and he reached into her body, ripping something away.

*My soul.*

She gasped, catapulting upright from her hotel room bed. "What the hell was that?"

# CHAPTER SEVEN

Forgetty had not returned to bed after the strange nightmare of the shadow man. Honestly, she didn't know what to make of it, but her best guess was that her mind had conjured the images and that they were a metaphor for the evil plague threatening to consume her.

Dressed in her white go-go dress and boots, her hair in its usual pigtail braids, she glanced at her hands as she took the elevator down to the lobby. Her fingertips felt ice cold, and her stomach wouldn't stop this horrible churning. Every cell in her body was fighting. *It's only a question of time now.*

Still, she was committed to searching for her mate until the bitter end. What other option was there? She wasn't permitted to give up even if she wished it—gods were hardwired to protect human-kind.

Once down in the lobby—an elegant, two-story space with an enormous crystal chandelier and bright white pillars—she looked around for her fellow DJs, only to find a man in a black suit holding a sign with a giant question mark.

*That must be for me. Perhaps the bus to the venue isn't running properly.* She walked up to the driver. "That's me."

"Good." He slid a card from his pocket and handed it to her.

"What's this?" Forgetty asked, inspecting the tiny envelope.

He shrugged.

She opened it and read the card, which said, *More than you'll ever know.*

*Wait.* Was this the same handwriting from the card last night that read "sorry"? *Sorry. More than you'll ever know.* That was what the two cards said when put together.

"Okay…" She looked at the man. "And who gave this to you?"

"Uhhh…" He rubbed his smooth chin, clearly unable to remember.

*The Forgetty side effect.*

"Never mind." She sighed. Whoever this was would reveal his or herself soon. Maybe it was just some crazy fan who kind of sort of remembered her. *And doesn't know how to write in complete sentences.*

Either way, she'd take the ride, which turned out to be a gleaming black limo.

*Nice,* she thought, stretching out in the backseat and helping herself to a glass of champagne. Not that material things truly impressed her. As a god, she'd amassed considerable wealth, which she used to fund various charities such as Alzheimer's research and ten different clinics that specialized in the care of humans who suffered from amnesia. She felt a special connection to her flock of mortals who no longer possessed the ability to remember. She understood their loneliness and frustration of not having control over one's life.

*Sucks pig toes.*

On the positive side, her circumstances had taught her to live in the moment. For example, a pleasant conversation with a kind stranger was simply that. No underlying motives, no judgment. It was simply a moment shared, enjoyed, and then gone. Sometimes, when working at her nightclubs, she would watch the masses stream onto the dance floor with heavy hearts, only to be freed from their worries by her presence. For those brief moments, their heartache would take a rest and they would remember how it felt to be happy. When the night was over, they'd return home to whatever fears consumed them, but she knew they would have renewed energy to resolve them, too.

So it wasn't all bad being her, but it was difficult.

*My burden to carry, I suppose.* Everyone had one. *Plus, I love music and being a DJ.* Music transcended time, generations, and in some cases, speech. It was the language of the soul. And, frankly, it was why her followers didn't really forget her. *The spirit doesn't forget. Not truly.*

The driver closed the door of the limo, enclosing her in the quiet, protective shell of the car, which was just what she needed before her big moment on stage. If she bombed again, she would crumple up into a sad little ball and die.

*Please, Universe, don't do this to me. I've been good to you and your flock. I've done everything you've asked.* Sadly, she just wasn't sure her voice had been heard.

*Guess I'll find out tonight.*

After checking in with her crew, who were all set to transition the stage over to her at exactly midnight, where she would spin for an hour and a half before the finale fireworks, Forgetty decided to take a different approach to her strategy tonight. This time, she would not stand on the stage until after her proposal. In addition, she would make sure the sound system distorted her voice to dampen the deific effect. It was much less likely that the crowd would become hypnotized and forgetful if they merely heard her voice through a synthesizer. In addition, they would not look at her directly prior to the show. A camera crew would show her image. She would use an artificial barrier, and if there were any interested males, they would be instructed to go to the side of the stage and given a backstage pass for the after-party. This way she would have many options to observe them with the other partygoers to determine if there was a connection.

*This time, it's going to work. I can feel it. He's out there tonight.* For gods' sake, this was Brazil, the land of hot men filled with passion.

"Miss…errr…" said the stagehand Waylon. "We are ready for that thing you asked us to do."

She gave him a polite nod, stowing her nerves down a deep dark hole. She pulled her braids forward and puckered her freshly glossed red lips.

With a deep inhale and thorough exhale, she looked at the two cameramen. "Ready."

They gave her a nod and started filming.

"Hello, my fellow—ugh!" Her body launched sideways, landing with a hard thud. Stunned, she vaguely heard the familiar, annoyingly deep male voice berating her, "Yet again, you're in my fucking way like a terminal moron."

She groaned, sensing a fracture in her ribs. "You again?"

"Your intelligence ceases to amaze me."

"Suuuck it," she groaned. "Hard."

"No. *You* suck it, you clumsy fool!"

She cracked open one eye. "Seriously, you body-check me for the third time, but I should suck it?"

He shrugged. "For the *third* time, you're trying to get my attention by stepping out of nowhere and colliding with me."

"As if!" She rolled to her side.

"As if? As if? I know your cheap little game, woman. If you only knew how many ladies try to get my attention with this breed of tricks."

Despite her pain, Forgetty managed to glance over her shoulder and give him the middle finger. "Bite me, dickhead."

"Uh, ma'am," said the cameraman, "do you want us to stop filming?"

Her eyes dashed to the giant lens pointed at her face. *Oh, dear gods of stupidity.* They had just broadcasted this entire little episode to fifty thousand people outside. "Turn it off!"

They did as she asked, and Waylon rushed over to help.

"Owww..." she whimpered, slowly getting to her feet as he gripped her bare elbow, realizing that too throbbed with pain.

"You all right?" asked Waylon.

"That loser roadie assaulted me for a third time."

"Which roadie?"

"The big one with the scowl and long hair."

Waylon frowned. "The guy wearing blue jeans and about yea tall?" He held up his hand a few inches above his own head.

"Yes. The one who acts like a bull in need of castration."

Waylon suddenly looked uncomfortable.

"What?" she prodded.

"That guy is—"

Suddenly, the stage manager—an English man with tatts galore, wearing torn black jeans—rushed over to them, screaming at the top of his lungs. "What the bloody hell is going on? I've got an empty stage over there, you twats!"

Forgetty looked at the man, wanting to tell him to also suck it, but he was right. We-J, who'd gone on before her, had left the stage minutes ago.

Forgetty let out a cranky breath. Her body hurt like hell, but she would heal fairly quickly. Yes, she needed to go out there and say something to the crowd.

*And I need to try one last time to find out if anyone might be compatible as my mate.* She was about to tell the camera crew to reset, but then the booing started. Tens of thousands of boos.

"Well? What the bloody hell are you waiting for, a spanking?" screamed the stage manager.

"Fine. I'm going!" Forgetty threw up her hands. "Put a spotlight on the stage and give me one minute before you start the introduction lights."

Everyone looked confused as she marched out to the elevated platform with the turntables and equipment. She swiped the microphone to the side and turned it on. "Testing?" She gave it a quick tap, immediately hearing her voice. "Hey, everyone! Good evening. Sorry about the delay, which I'm sure you'll all forget about in five seconds, but I have a favor." The arena fell silent, fifty thousand faces glued to her.

*Dammit, if I get rejected again, this is gonna suck.* But she still had that nagging sensation in her gut that he was out there tonight.

"Okay, this sounds strange, I know, but I'm looking for love. So if any guy out there feels something powerful enough not to forget what I've just said, please…" Her voice faded as she felt a set of angry blue eyes drilling into her. Slowly, she turned her head to see the mean-ass roadie glaring at her, his muscled tattooed arms crossed defiantly over his broad chest, his feet apart.

"Hey, second time is a charm. Don't let me stop you, woman."

*Ohmygod…* The mic slipped from her hand. *He remembers me. He remembers!* Like a frying pan in the face, it dawned on her that moments earlier, he had said the word *third*. *His exact words: "For the third time, you're trying to get my attention…"* blah, blah, blah.

Staring at him in utter disbelief, her mouth fell open. *Oh…come. On! This brute?* Sure, he was a nice-looking male specimen on the outside, but lordy! Hands down, he was the biggest prick she'd ever met. He was also the first male to ever remember her, aside from her siblings, who only held vague recollections of her (except for Acan). But never in seventy thousand years had a non-deity recalled her.

*I can't believe this crap.* But as she stood there, locking eyes with this bastard of a roadie, there was no denying the truth: He was smirking, once again enjoying her public humiliation.

*I so hate you, Universe.*

She pulled her eyes away from him and stared out across the ocean of blank faces, opening all of her senses to the energy flowing through the air, hoping to gods that the feeling from earlier—the one telling her that *he* was out there—would lead to a different answer.

*Please be there. Please be there.* A sharp tug in her stomach toward stage left led her gaze straight back to Mr. Nasty's bitter scowl and electric blue eyes.

*Great. Just great. I get to decide between destroying the world or hooking up with this jerk face.*

"Oi! Move your buns, missy!" the stage manager screamed.

With a snarl on her lips, she stepped off the platform, marched straight toward Mr. Blue Eyes, and stopped two feet in front of him.

"What are you doing?" he growled. "You have a show to put on."

"You," she pointed to his face, "will be silent."

He frowned in question.

She reached up and pulled his head to hers, planting a lingering kiss on his lips. To her surprise, it felt kind of good. *Warm, soft, sensual lips.* Very surprising.

She snapped her head back and pointed in his face. "Okay, soft lips, you will meet me at my hotel room after the event."

He cocked one dark brow. "Why would I do that?"

"Because if you do not, I will hunt you down,

remove your beautiful smooth olive skin that seems to be well moisturized despite your rough manly exterior, and then I will dismember you, starting with that foul tongue."

His snarl slowly melted away. "What kind of man can resist such an offer?" A slow, wicked smile crept over those soft lips. Lips that had also been cruel and deployed offensive words requiring punishment—just as soon as she sorted all this out. She refused to believe that he was *the one. Silky lips or not.*

"Good," she said. "I'm staying at—"

"I know where you're staying," he said in a smug tone. "I'm paying for your room. Now do as my stage manager has requested and get your buns back to work." He turned and walked away, full of piss and vinegar. And swagger. Lots of swagger.

Forgetty slowly turned, feeling gut punched. *Mr. Liath? Ohmygods. I should've known.*

# CHAPTER EIGHT

After Forgetty's final performance, an awesome lineup of Frank Sinatra mashed up with Cold Play and house tracks she'd personally laid down, she skipped the after-party—no males had taken up her offer—and headed back to the hotel.

*I can't believe this,* she thought, reality finally sinking in. Basically, the one man on the planet she found offensive and did not want to get to know was the one man the Universe had comically (and sadistically) pushed her towards.

*No. I just don't believe it.* Which was why she needed to interrogate him. This had to be a mistake. Some huge, hideous mistake. *'Cause no way am I letting that douchebag bed me. Not for all the tea in China.*

She growled at herself, knowing that was a lie. The Universe had hardwired her to save humans whether she liked it or not, and that meant, at the very least, attempting to have a civil conversation with this Mr. Liath in order to ascertain if he truly could be her mate—*pfft! Not likely.* What sort of man knocked a woman down and then yelled at her and walked away.

She slid on a soft black hoodie dress with a big pocket in the front. It was the sort of outfit that said, *I'm not going to bother looking good for you because you're not worth it.*

And what was with him hiding who he was? All right, maybe he wasn't hiding, but he certainly behaved like a roadie and dressed like a roadie. He hadn't made his identity known. *And he sure the hell isn't in his sixties.* Where had that BS rumor come from?

At three in the morning, there was a hard knock on the door of her hotel room. She walked over and peeked through the tiny hole.

*Liath.* Her blood pressure instantly spiked and her lips tingled with the recollection of that kiss.

She pasted on a sugary smile and opened the door. "Well, well, Mr. Liath. Nice of you to make it."

She stepped aside, allowing him to pass before closing the door.

He made his way over to the living room, which was a considerable size with a plush khaki sofa and armchair and stained-glass coffee table. An enormous flat-screen in the corner sat lifeless, but she had the curtains open to display a spectacular view of Rio's sparkling coastline.

"Nice place. Hope you're enjoying it," he said with a stark tone.

He took a seat, his impressive seven-foot frame taking up almost half of the three-person sofa.

Forgetty's eyes twitched with suspicion as she attempted to puzzle him out.

She walked over and took the armchair angled toward the corner of the coffee table. "So—"

"Make it quick, sweetheart. I have things to do."

She jerked her head back in shock. "Well, then go do them."

His blue eyes narrowed. "You asked me here—no. That's incorrect. You demanded I come."

"I did, but I won't put up with your buffoonery and piggery and general ickiness. By the way, why did you not tell me who you are?"

"Why would I? You were paid, travel taken care of, and you DJed at ten of my events. None of these required you and I have a direct relationship."

"It's sketchy, that's why. Anyone running a large international event like that would be interested in making sure things run smoothly."

"I have people I pay for that."

She wasn't getting anywhere with this man. *Okay. Think, think…what do I really want to know?* As her mind stirred, her eyes drifted to his muscular thighs encased in new black leather pants.

*Hmm… He changed his clothes from earlier.* He even wore a white, nicely starched shirt with little black buttons. *Looks expensive.* She then noted how his plentiful pecs swelled against the fabric and a smattering of dark hair peeked out between the lapels of his collar.

"Well," he stood, filling the room with his intimidating presence, "this has been a complete waste of time."

*Huh?* She jerked to her feet. "Wait."

"For what?" He speared her with his ice blue eyes.

"I…I want to know why you remember me?"

He looked at her like she was stupid. "You brought me here to feed your ego? You really are a moron."

"Okay, buddy! I've had it with that mouth of yours." She stepped toward him, determined to give him a big jolt of god juice.

She reached out and let 'er rip. He flew back with a grunt, landing right on the sofa.

"Ow! What the fuck?" he groaned.

"Insult me one more time. I dare you," she snarled, stepping closer and bending down to meet his gaze.

Their noses ten inches apart, she stared into his eyes, and a strange sensation washed over her. She suddenly felt—not heard but *felt*—his heartbeat thrumming away. She felt it like a river of warm vibrations coursing through her veins, gripping every cell of her being and lulling them, igniting them.

Her eyes went wide. "What. Is. That?"

"What is what?"

"Don't tell me you don't feel it."

With a dry, emotionless face, he said, "I don't feel it."

"Lying jerk."

His right eye twitched. "Bitch."

"Asshole."

"God, I so want to throw you down on the floor and fuck you."

"Ha!" She jumped up and pointed in his face. "I knew it! I knew it! You ran into me on purpose. You kept knocking me down because you just wanted me on the ground, probably with my knees hooked around your big, strong shoulders while you fucked me breathless with your big dick." She paused. "It is big, isn't it?"

A sly smile curved one side of his sinful mouth. "Huge."

Images of him plowing into her, his strong body over her, in her, heating her, pummeled her mind. *Dear gods, he is so beautiful*—the magnificent size of him, the long thick hair, the angular jaw covered in a short dark beard that called out to her fingertips and begged for a proper petting.

*Wait. Nuh-uh.* She stepped back, feeling flustered and filled with aching need. *This guy does not get to have me. I deserve a good man. A man who protects me, cherishes me, and remembers me.* He only checked one of those boxes.

"You need to go." She jerked her head toward the door.

"Huh?" Now *he* looked sucker punched.

She took several more steps away from him, the sofa, and the coffee table. "Out. Now."

"It's my room."

She lifted her brows. "Sorry?"

"I paid for this room. Technically it's mine. Therefore, you cannot ask me to leave."

"Wait. A second ago, I had to stop you from going, and now you want to stake a claim?"

He toggled his head from side to side. "No. Not really. I was merely making a point."

"Ohhh-kay. You really need to go. Now." She pointed toward the door.

"I never should've come here. Not when I know what you're after." He drew a breath, causing his large chest to expand. "You're like all the rest."

*What the hell!* He made it sound like she was some giant horny goddess toad. "Sex is never a motive for my actions. I've never even had a relationship, which you heard me announce publically."

"I'm not surprised. Who would want someone like you?"

*Okay, that one hurt.* She knew she wasn't relationship material, because one had to form a connection with another person for that to be true, but he'd made it sound like she was worthless.

*The one man in the world who remembers me, though I do not know why, and he literally turds on me. After physically assaulting me.* What sort of cruel game was the Universe playing? Was he supposed to be a lesson? Because she didn't see a learning moment in this. Yet, she felt a connection. It would explain why he kept showing up and colliding physically with her. The Universe demanded they notice each other. *Or he subconsciously really does want me on the ground for kinky, dirty sex.* Or perhaps both?

*Who cares!* She'd served loyally for seventy millennia. This could not be what the Universe was asking of her: To choose between her self-esteem and happiness or the entire human race? Because faced with such a decision, she would have to choose the seven-plus billion souls on the planet, not counting the furry masses and sea turtles, over her own life, which essentially was what this all boiled down to.

*Mr. Hottie McJerkface or…everyone? Ugh! I hate my existence.*

"You're a real gentleman, Mr. Liath." She looked away, forcing her eyes to remain dry.

Considering his major assholiness, she expected him to leave, but instead she heard him draw a deep breath, almost the sort one might take when filled with regret.

"I'm sorry," he said, "more than you'll ever know." He walked over to the door and left.

Forgetty stood there for several moments before his words kicked in. Her head whipped toward the door. *"Sorry. More than you'll ever know"?* He was flowers/limo guy.

Something told her that things were not as they seemed, that *he* was not as he seemed. She sprinted for the door, pulled it open and ran toward the elevators, hoping to catch him. As she skidded around the corner in her bare feet, she spotted him stepping inside.

"Wait!" She ran as fast as her bare feet could carry her, sliding into the elevator right as the doors shut.

His eyes met hers, and she stared into his. "Tell me the truth. Who are you? Why do you remember me?"

"Kiss me again."

She instantly felt her lips tingle with desire. "What? No. And I asked you a question."

"Have dinner with me tomorrow night."

She blinked at him. "And then what?" She needed answers because none of this was adding up. He was the biggest dick she'd ever met. And a closet romantic who felt the need to apologize for a reason unbeknownst to her.

"Then we see." He leaned past her, providing the opportunity to take a delicious whiff of his freshly washed body and rich spicy cologne. He pushed the button for the next floor and then stepped back.

As they exchanged looks, the elevator slowed and the doors slid open.

"This is your stop. I'll pick you up at eight," he said with that deep hard tone lacking warmth and heavy on the alpha male.

It dawned on her; this man was used to having

his orders followed without question. Yes, he sounded like a general. She could see a resemblance between him and her brother Votan, the God of Death and War—the uncompromising arrogance, the lack of empathy, the utterly bizarre way of showing affection. Like a giant emotional moron.

Deciding they'd gotten as far as they could for the moment, she stepped off the elevator and faced him. They locked eyes, her heart thundering away inside her chest, until the silver doors cut them off.

"Wow." She released a hot breath, placing her fingertips to her hot needy lips. "That was intense." Add weird and so very confusing. But tomorrow night, she would get to his bottom—*I mean him. The bottom of him. I mean, of this.*

Yet, somehow, she sensed that the masculine enigma with a hard-as-hell disposition in that elevator was a man with a dark past. Yes, every cell in her body confirmed it. He was dangerous, lethal, and not who he said.

*And I think I have to date him to save the world.*

# CHAPTER NINE

Zac, God of Temptation and the most evil mother-fucking badass deity on the planet, sat in the basement jail cell on the Island of El Corazón, contemplating his next move. Soon, Tula would come to set him free, and then the fun would begin.

Step one: flee island with Tula.

Step two: take Tula somewhere secluded.

Step three: break her or kill her. Perhaps both?

Step four: return to El Corazón and take revenge on these fucking annoying mermen.

*Step five: live happily ever after in a cloud of delusions and darkness because the one woman on the planet I love more than anything, who is so good, so pure, so loving that another like her will never exist again, and it makes me feel horribly guilty to even think of harming her because it merely validates that I have indeed lost my mind and succumbed to the plague*—deep breath—*I know that destroying her will destroy me.*

Zac's black heart swelled with despair. This violent deity wasn't him, and he somehow knew it despite being encased by a blanket of sickness.

*Jesus. I can't allow her to free me.* Tula had to

run.

"Zac!" Tula's sweet voice filled the underground room.

Zac got to his feet, his entire body electrified with a potent combination of fear and sadistic hunger. "Tula, do not come down here. Whatever you do!"

Her panicked, sweet face appeared in the stairwell. "Why? What happened?"

"You must go! You cannot free me."

She rushed toward him. "What did they do to you, Zac?"

*Dear gods, why won't she listen?* "They have done nothing. But you are not safe around me and, therefore, cannot set me free."

Through the bars, her innocent blue eyes gazed up at him. "Zac," she said in a hushed voice, "whatever they have done to you, whatever lies Cimil has told you—I won't let it stand. I know in my heart you will not harm me. I said as much when Minky kidnapped me and brought me here."

"She was right to do so," he growled. "Because if you only knew the horrible things I plan to do once I am free, you'd understand that I must be tossed to the bottom of the ocean."

Tula's sweet pink lips smiled with tenderness as she produced a set of keys. "Mr. Zac, you know I don't like to swear, but my mamma didn't raise no fool, so wake the hell up." She shoved one key into the lock and began turning.

"No! Tula! Do not do—"

*Click! Click!* The door swung out, and Tula extended her hand. "Come, Zac. I love you, and you have to trust it will be okay."

His entire body shaking, he wanted to reach out to her, but the part of him that loved her wouldn't allow it. The part of him that wanted to do harm, however?

He rushed for her, his large hands threading through her soft golden locks. He pulled her toward him and gazed down into her eyes. "I'm going to hurt you, Tula."

"You mean you forgot to bring black jade? Because I didn't." She held up a shiny black ring on her pinkie.

"That is not what I mean, but where'd you get that?"

"Minky." She flashed a loving, confident smile. "Now kiss me and accept that it was always you. You were meant for me, and nothing else matters."

Hungry for her taste and touch, Zac bent his head and pressed his lips to her warm mouth. Their tongues collided. Their bodies melted into each other. Their souls reached through the darkness, clawing at one another. His arms snaked around her petite frame, pressing the two of them tightly together. *Gods, she feels so good, so right.*

"I love you, Tula," he whispered between the fury of lapping tongues and sinful groans.

"I love you, too."

Suddenly, everything around him ignited in a bright light. As if someone had pulled the stopper bottling up all that rage and darkness, Zac felt the poisons draining from his soul, replaced by Tula's pure light.

*What is happening?* All of the darkness had evaporated, leaving behind only a longing to never part from her. And just like that, he finally understood why she had been brought into his life; she was never meant to belong to him. He was meant to belong to her—to serve her, to keep her safe, to shield her pure soul from the wickedness that tempted all living creatures. The Universe had created her for a reason, and Cimil had been right; Tula was special, though he didn't know why. He simply felt it deep inside every molecule of his being. And there was no one more suited to protect her than the God of Temptation, who understood all the threats the world had to offer.

He broke the kiss and stepped back. "No. Stop." As much as he desired her and loved her, as much as he ached for contact, no one could be allowed to threaten Tula's innocence and purity. It was what made her special and allowed her to look past his flaws and love him unconditionally.

*Fucking hell. I can't ever bed her.* Irony at its finest. She was his ultimate temptation. But if he wanted her love, he could not change her. He could only protect her.

"Zac? What's the matter? Why did you stop

kissing me?" Tula asked sweetly.

"We'll discuss it later. Right now, we must run and get the hell off this island." He reached for her hand, and she quickly jerked it away.

"Do you plan on killing me, or are you cured?" she asked.

He looked at her with the deepest affection. "I am cured."

"Then why do you still have that look on your face, like you want to kill someone?"

He blinked. "Because I may have to do so in order for us to leave this place; we cannot stay." The mermen were about to sink his ass to the bottom of the ocean. And then who would protect Tula? He was the only one capable. The *only* one.

"Please don't kill any more, Zac. Not even to save my life—I'm begging you." She reached for his hand.

He smiled softly, unable to deny her anything. Except the truth. "Yes, my sweet mortal. I will not kill anyone," he lied. "Now let us go before they discover I'm free."

ॐ ॐ

Cimil stood at the foot of her custom-made, XXL bed in her three-story mansion overlooking Hollywood, staring at her mate, Roberto. She loved the way he slept, with his strong arms crossed over his chest, his tall body stretched out like a plank, a golden staff in his hand.

*Pharaohs. So adorable.* She would have to get his favorite snack this morning—bloody Mary. Mary was one of Roberto's many snack buddies. She had buckteeth, no common sense, and a general miserableness that could turn off the horniest of men, vampires included. But Roberto loved her bitter blood.

Cimil left the room and headed down the hallway, where her four children remained snug in their little coffins. They were only half vampire, but they really got a kick out of role-playing, and lately they'd all decided to be Dracula.

*So cute. My personal little horror show pets!* But not forever. Eventually, the Universe would right herself, and Cimil's babies would turn good. *Mostly. After all, I am their mother.*

As she took the spiral staircase down, Cimil's phone vibrated in her bright fuzzy yellow bathrobe. "Hey-low!"

"Cimil! It is I, Roen. Your brother has escaped with the girl."

"What the furry fartsicles?" She tripped and tumbled down the stairs, landing on the tile floor with a loud thump. "Ouch!"

"Cimil, this is no time for your games."

"I know that! Annual Stumble Down Stairs Day was last month. Ugh! I think I broke something."

"Ask me if I care."

"Do you care?" *Please say yes. I'm feeling needy.*

"No."

*Jerk!*

"Cimil," he added, "I don't know what you are planning, but we will not rest until your brother is caught and punished."

"Now you ask me if I care," she replied. Because she'd say no, and then who'd feel stupid now?

"Where is Zac, Cimil?" Roen growled. "And no more bullshit because we have your unicorn. If you ever want to see her again, you will find your brother and return him to our island."

"What the hell! You have Minky?" Cimil couldn't believe this.

"After what you did last Easter, we know not to trust you and needed insurance."

"I got confused. I thought your home was Easter Egg Island, so I hid some eggs. Big whoop!" Besides, where was their sense of fun?

"Those were bombs."

She rolled her eyes. "Pussy."

"What did you just call me?"

"Nothing you weren't already called five times before breakfast by your woman. Now give me back my Minky or I will bring a storm of destruction to your doorstep that's so furious you'll think your asshole is the nicest place on the planet."

"That makes no sense. Why would I ever think that?" he said blandly.

Then it dawned on her that if the nearly unintelligible garble she'd heard from the dead was correct, then in seven days none of this would matter. She would forget who she was and all about Minky.

"Fine. You win. But don't feed her after midnight, and make sure she never gets wet."

"I'm fairly sure you're speaking of a gremlin."

"Yeah, Minky's dad was a badass. Gotta go!" She ended the call, thinking over her decision. In all honesty, what could she do without her powers, which allowed her to sift through the billions of voices of the dead? Without her gifts, she couldn't extract critical details from the masses, some of whom were the dead from future—*'cause, yanno. We all gotta die sometime.* She'd even spoken to her dead self a few times to avoid the apocalypse. But without her powers, the dead just sounded like a room full of clowns with their red noses on fire—lots of screams and honking. No help at all.

*Wait.* That was it. She needed to be helpful again and get her powers back. *That's right. Enough with this whole penance bull-cocky.* She was a goddess vital to the planet's survival.

However, to get her powers back, she'd have to gather the gods for an emergency summit. *And I know what they'll say: Another apocalyptic event? That's the fifth one this century, Cimil, and we're not buying it.*

But she wasn't helpless. No. She had a secret weapon she'd kept for such an occasion: thousands of years of blackmail material, the kind that would result in epic humiliation. For example, one of her brothers had a seven-inch penis.

*Ha! If that got out, he'd never be able to show his face again.* They'd call him cheese doodle dick or Gerkinstein. *Or worse…human male dick!* Oh, the shame to be so small.

Another one of her brothers still slept with a nightlight.

Yes, there were plenty of shameful, embarrassing photos, videos, and letters she could use to blackmail them all and bend them to her will. All she needed was a majority vote of the fourteen gods. So, counting herself and Forgetty—a shoo-in—she only needed six more votes.

"Minky! Take me to my piggy bank!" The famous piggy bank was a secret vault hidden in the jungles of the Yucatan, where she kept her most valuable items—her ThighMaster, her favorite fuzzy pink socks, her entire collection of *Love Boat* episodes. "And my blackmail box!"

Cimil waited for the whoosh of wind and to be whisked away, but it didn't come.

*Dangit!* She'd forgotten Minky was with the mermen. "How am I ever going to get to Mexico and save the world? Again."

"I can take you, my love." Roberto stood in his black boxers, holding his golden staff. "I can sift you there and be back before the kids are up."

"What would I do without you?" Cimil sighed contentedly.

"You would go mad, move into a tree, and start wearing a diaper because you believe you're a monkey—like my old uncle Ibi did when my aunt left him."

"Poor Ibi." Cimil shook her head. "I can't ever lose you. Let's go."

"May I first inquire as to what glorious perils we face this week?" Roberto asked, scratching his manly kiwis through his underwear.

"Oh, you know, the usual. Forgetty is about to flip, and we're all going to experience worldwide senility and a collapse of civilization."

"Oooh…exciting." His dark eyes flickered with enthusiasm.

"Right?" She stared up at him, her chest heaving with joyful breaths. "Honestly, I love that you get me."

"And I love that you love that I get you. Now let us watch the world dip its toe into the waters of demise once more."

"You know, there's a real chance I can't save us this time," Cimil pointed out happily. "Especially if I can't convince my brethren to return my powers."

"Even better. I love a challenge. Now let us sift to Mexico, and remind me to bring back coconuts. Today I am going to teach our evil seeds the fine art of cracking skulls with one's thighs."

Cimil clapped and bounced on the balls of her feet! "Oh! I completely forgot that skull-cracking day is next week." She gave him a look. "Seriously,

Roberto, I just want to transport you back in time so you can reshape the world into a glorious conga line of violent, offensive, and obscure holidays."

He sifted to her and held her fast to his manly body. "The first day of every month would belong to you, my love. I would call it Bat-shit Crazy Day. It would require all to wear bat shit and speak in pig Latin, as is required on your birthday."

Her heartbeat accelerated like a hummingbird on Red Bull. "Godsdammit, I love you," she growled. "Let's make four new babies."

"We've been trying for months."

She gave him a wink. "I have a good feeling about this one. My ovaries are tingly."

"You know just how to get me excited. My seed is yours."

# CHAPTER TEN

Forgetty had spent a solid ten minutes getting ready for her date with the mysterious Mr. Liath, who was nearly an hour late.

*He'd better have a damned good excuse.* Sitting on the khaki couch, wearing her favorite yellow minidress and white boots, she folded her arms over her chest. She'd never been stood up. Not once.

*All right, I've never actually been on a real date either, since demons don't count, but that only adds salt to the wound.* Her dating journey would be forever tainted by this.

She reached for the TV remote sitting on the glass end table and flipped to the news. Perhaps there was a major accident? Or a terrorist threat? *Or maybe he got cold feet.*

She tried not to laugh at the thought. With his enormous ego, he was far too full of himself to permit any weakness in his life. She bet a man like him had never experienced so much as a cold toe. *Or even a chilly nut sack on a January morn'.*

*Knock. Knock!*

She swiveled on the couch and glared at the doorway. "That'd better be him." Because if it was turndown service, the poor bed fluffer was about to meet a nasty end.

Forgetty stood, smoothing down the front of her polyester blend dress, and marched to the door.

She opened it and froze, finding not a man, but a sex god—no, no. Not her brother Chaam. *This…this is a warrior in a tailored suit*—sleek, handsome, and deadly. Okay, that last part she'd guessed, but he looked the part. Who knew that Mr. Liath cleaned up so nicely?

*Yeah, but he's still late, and that's just not acceptable.*

Forgetty perched a fist on her hip. "And just where the hell have you been, huh?"

He arched one dark brow, producing a bouquet of red roses.

"Thanks, but no. Already have some." She crossed her arms. "And do you really think that's going to win me over when you're an hour late?"

With a ramrod-straight back and a firm tug on his black tie with his free hand, he looked her in the eyes. "No. But the fact I am ten minutes early, wearing an expensive suit designed to impress you, and bearing a gift of flowers should warm you up."

*Ten minutes early?* Her eyes crawled to the clock on the wall to her right, which displayed seven fifty. *Oh, jeez. Someone please icepick me in the temple and send me back to my realm.* She'd apparently been so excited to find out what or who he was that she'd misread the clock.

"Hey." He reached for her hand. "It's okay. You were really looking forward to seeing me. You're not the first."

She jerked her hand away. "Slight overstatement, bud."

He shrugged his broad shoulders. "Deny it all you want. I won't make fun of you when you whimper for my touch and expert lovemaking."

Her jaw dropped. "Wow. I have nothing to say to that. Nothing at all."

"To the contrary; I believe 'wow' says it all." He held out his arm. "Shall we?"

She remained motionless, contemplating what any goddess might. *Save planet, humans, and tiny furry creatures or…smoosh chauvinistic pig.*

*Smoosh! Smoosh!*

Sadly, they were empty words. Her purpose was to serve humans just as she always had. On the bright side, however, she had endured far worse than this man. If he turned out to be her mate, she would survive. *I will pluck out my own eardrums so I don't have to hear his bull crap, but I will survive.* She would leave in her eyes, because he wasn't bad to look at.

She pasted on a sour smile. "Where are we going?"

"It's a surprise."

"Sounds terrifying." She took his arm.

༄ ༄

*Ten seconds later...*

"Ummm...you're taking me on a date to your hotel room next door to mine?" And he'd been staying there the entire time? *WTH?*

He unlocked the door and held it open for her. "It has the best view in Rio, and the five-star chef has prepared a meal that rivals anything found in Paris, New York, or Memphis."

Forgetty gave that last one some thought. "Memphis?"

"I'm into barbeque, especially cooking over an open fire pit—sort of a long-standing tradition in my family. I enjoy fresh raw meat, too."

*Yuck.* "I suppose barbeque is tasty, but raw meat is for animals. Tell me, are you an animal?" Because she still had no idea what he was.

"In bed, yes. And I like your enthusiasm." He jerked his head, gesturing for her to enter his suite. "Shall we continue with dinner, then? I, too, am anxious to fuck you."

Her turquoise eyes nearly sprang from her head. "Huh?"

"This is the reason you agreed to this date, is it not? I see no point in beating around the bush, considering what and who you are."

Forgetty rapidly blinked, her heartrate amping. She was unsure if she should address his lack of chivalry or the comment pertaining to *who/what* she was.

*Decisions, decisions.*

She shoved him inside, catching him off guard.

He stumbled back with a grunt. "Hey!"

"First," she held out her index finger and slammed the door shut behind her, "you're an insensitive bastard bordering on cruel."

"And you're pointing out this obvious fact because…?"

"Because you are *so* not getting in my pants."

"I hardly think my honesty is an adequate reason not to let me fuck you."

"How about you have no manners and you've physically assaulted me three times. I can only imagine how horrible you'd be in bed." He'd likely pound on her until he came and then push her out of the bed with his feet and tell her to get lost.

"I am excellent in bed. Especially if you're a fan of angry sex, which I suspect you might be, considering your age and the fact you're still a virgin. I would be pretty angry, too."

*Uh! Wha! He did not go there!* "Wait. How old do you think I am?"

"Seventy thousand years, give or take," he replied confidently.

*He knows I'm a goddess.* "Who are you?"

He gave her the strangest of looks, like she was thickheaded for even asking.

"What?" she barked.

He began opening his mouth just as the door flew open. In the short hallway stood a young man, likely about sixteen, with brown eyes, long brown hair, and a wild look in his eyes.

"Louie…" Mr. Liath snarled. "Where the hell have you been?"

Off the bat, Forgetty realized that this Louie's energy was dark and so horrifically violent that she felt compelled to step back. She'd never seen a person with such an ominous aura.

*Well, okay. Except for the Maaskab.* The Maaskab were those ancient evil Mayan priests who excelled in the dark arts and had single-handedly wiped out their own people. Manufactured plagues, human sacrifices, ritualistic experimentation—they'd systematically destroyed the most advanced civilization of the time because they were thirsty for power. And because they were just plain old assholes. Then, hundreds of years later, they would team up with evil vampires around the world and attempt to enslave mankind. If it hadn't been for Cimil's hubby, Roberto—the vampire king—stepping in and killing off the entire evil vampire bloodline, the world today would be a vastly different place. In the end, however, the Maaskab were all but completely wiped out. Cimil had kept a handful alive for educational purposes—those guys knew a lot about harnessing supernatural energy for things like time travel, and they were even responsible for the gods being able to mate. Black jade had originally been a Maaskab discovery.

*So why does this kid have their aura?*

Mr. Liath pointed a menacing finger in the young man's face. "You will answer me, Louie."

Louie narrowed his dark eyes. "Fuck you, loser."

*Whoa! Someone give him a time-out!*

"Loser." Liath's blue eyes twitched with rage. "Well, the apple doesn't fall very far from the tree, *son*," he spat.

*Gasp! Louie is Liath's son? Why do I feel like I just walked into the middle of someone else's telenovela? This is freakin' juicy. I'd better catch up!*

She turned to Louie, who looked like he'd been punched in the gut and wanted to tear off Mr. Liath's head. "But…but you said—"

"Yeah. I know what I said," Liath seethed, "and it was a fucking lie. So deal with it. And while you're doing that, mind your tongue, boy, or I'll cut it from your head."

"Jesus!" Forgetty cringed. "That's a bit much. And, btw, you're so never, ever getting laid by me after talking to him like that—not that you had a chance."

"My name is Távas, not Jesus. And shut that mouth of yours, woman, or I will bend you over my knee. I care not that you are a goddess."

*Whoa-the-fuck-whoa. Someone slap my goddess cheek and feed me a get-the-fuck-out yogurt with whoa-the-fuck-whoa sprinkles.*

"Where do you get off speaking to me like that, you crusty turd, and how the hell do you know so much about me?" she asked.

"That is no concern of yours—"

A rush of sirens broke his train of thought. He turned his head to the empty doorway. "Where is Louie?"

"Duh." Forgetty huffed. "He probably ran for the hills because you're a complete assh—"

Faint human screams erupted off in the distance. It sounded as though they were coming from outside, down on the street.

Mr. Liath—Távas—whatever—turned ghost white and bolted to one of the two bedroom windows. Within seconds, he could be heard belting out the WTFs and holy hells.

Forgetty rushed to the window where Távas stood, leaning outside.

*Dear gods! The kid is on the ledge!* Forgetty turned sideways and squeezed out the window, which was almost entirely taken up by Távas's large body.

"You fucking lied to me!" Louie yelled, his face wet with tears.

Forgetty's divine blood turned to icicles. *This juicy telenovela just became an episode of every parent's worst nightmare.* From what she could tell, this young man really wanted to jump. And though she had absolutely no clue what she'd walked into, she knew that Távas was terrified. She could smell the fear on him.

But why had he been so harsh with the young man if he cared so much? Perhaps no one had ever taught this man how to show kindness, because clearly he understood the concept—as proven by his awkward attempt to woo her with flowers, the suit, the limo, and nice hotel rooms.

"Louie," Távas yelled with that menacing voice, "if you kill yourself, I will remove your head and beat it like a stupid piñata!"

*You prove my point.* Távas was about as compassionate as a fart.

"I don't want to be your son," Louie blubbered. "And you don't want to be my father. I can't live like this anymore."

"Like what?" Forgetty jumped on Louie's words.

"Silence!" Távas pushed her back. "This is between my son and me. Return to your room."

Forgetty's right eye twitched, and her nostrils flared. *Do not push Távas out that window. Do not push Távas out that window. Dear gods, I think I'm going to push him out that wind—no!* She had to keep her cool. Távas was the only guy on the planet who remembered her, and like it or not, he might very well be the key to saving her from flipping.

"Távas," she said in a level voice, "if you know who I am, then you know I can help. And I can see that you care about your son, which is why I do not have to tell you that the best thing for you to do is step aside."

Facing out the window, she watched Távas's large, muscled frame stiffen, followed by his broad shoulders rising with the weight of a burdened breath.

"Távas?" she urged, gently squeezing his arm through his suit jacket. "Please move before it is too late."

Without looking at her, he turned away. "I will wait in the living room."

He disappeared, and Forgetty drew a soul-steadying breath before bellying up to the sill.

Louie looked checked out, his dark eyes locked onto the street below, where squad cars lit up the night. Onlookers gathered on the sidewalk across the way.

She didn't have much experience with such situations, but being a DJ to the masses who sought escape, she easily recognized the look of destitution in his eyes. He had nothing to live for.

"Louie," she said quietly, "I'm Getty. And very few people know this about me, but I'm *just* like you."

His gaze remained fixed on the street. "Doubtful."

"I live every day feeling like I'm invisible, like I could disappear from the face of the planet and no one would notice. But that's a lie. I'm here for a reason, and without me, the world just wouldn't be the same."

"You're trying to make me feel better." Louie sniffled.

"Sadly, I am not. I live on the fringes of the world, in the shadows of people's minds. It's very lonely, but I take comfort in knowing that I still have a purpose. So do you."

"What?" he scoffed. "To be a loser like my dad?"

"No. No one defines you but you, Louie. You get to shape your life. But it's up to you to do the work and find your path."

He flashed a hard look. "That sounds like some bullshit poster at a new age shop."

She bobbed her head. "Yet you find yourself knowing it to be true. The Universe is complex, insane, and chaotic, but she doesn't make mistakes." *Except for mating me to Távas. Huge fumble, Universe. Huge!*

"So I was meant to be a bad person who's done bad things. I was meant to hurt people even when I didn't want to."

No. But she could see that he'd been infected with the sort of darkness that now threatened her. How? Why? What was Távas's connection to this? She wasn't sure, but this wasn't the moment to find all that out. She just needed him to get down off the ledge. Preferably on the inside of the hotel room.

"Oh gods." She laughed, trying to make him feel better. "Is that what this is about? You hurt a few people?"

"Maybe."

"Pfft. You should meet my sister Cimil. In a million years, you couldn't come close to the horrible things she's done, but you know what? She never gives up trying to do her best. Not even on Fridays, when she calls herself *Biaaanca*. Basically, her evil day. But she still tries to be her best evil self and find a way to make it work for humanity." Murdering evildoers and all that.

Forgetty zeroed in on Louie's gloomy face. She hadn't gotten through to him. Whatever malevolent energy had wrapped itself around his heart, it was a sticky son of a bitch and would require time to dissolve. Kind of like crispy catsup on the edges of the meatloaf dish.

*Gods, I love meatloaf.* It was the first dish she learned to cook after she'd decided that she would live a full life, even if it was to be alone. Comfort food had been number two on her list of things to conquer. Number one had been sex.

*Still working on number one.*

"Okay, Louie. Just look me in the eyes and tell me why the world is a better place without you. Convince me, and I'll let you jump. Hell, I'll give you a push."

Half shocked, half confused, he stared her in the eyes. "Because if that man is my father, there is no hope for me."

She tipped her head to one side. *Huh?*

Suddenly, Louie began leaning forward.

"No!" She lunged for his hand and released her goddess energy.

# CHAPTER ELEVEN

*What a blur. A horrible, scary blur.* Forgetty had never been through anything like this. As Louie lunged and she pulsed with her forgetfulness, the world stood still. In one hand, Louie's wrist. In the other, Távas's hand held onto hers, her body dangling over the cement sidewalk.

"Do not let go, goddess." Távas strained under their weight.

"Not on your pigheaded life," she growled. It wasn't that she feared crashing to her death—it would hurt, but she couldn't really die—however, his son would not survive the fall.

"Hang on." Távas groaned, pulling her up an inch at a time, police sirens blazing in the night, seeming to come from every direction.

"I'm hanging on every word!" she yelled, knowing that Louie was out cold from the burst of light she'd given him. It would wear off by tomorrow, and by then, she would have gotten to the bottom of all this.

With a few heaves and hoes, Távas had them both through the window and back onto solid ground.

He laid Louie on the bed just as there was a loud knock at the door. He turned and grabbed Forgetty by the shoulders. "Are you all right?"

She gave him a nod.

"Good. Then let me do the talking." He went to answer the door, and within seconds the *policia de Rio* were in the room, inspecting Louie and pulling her and Távas to the living room for questioning. She could see in Távas's eyes that he wanted to go to his son and did not appreciate their strong-arm tactics.

"No." She grabbed Távas's hand, sending a spike of warmth through her arm. It almost felt intimate, which shocked the hell out of her, frankly. "Best let them do their thing and leave. We don't want trouble."

"Can you not simply use your gifts so they will feel confused and leave?" he whispered into her ear.

She gazed out the panoramic window at the dark ocean, mulling it over. Typically, she didn't use her powers unless absolutely necessary; however, this was no ordinary situation. The clock was ticking on her sitch. *I really need to find out who Távas is before my weasel pops.*

"I suppose," she replied, "I could. But once they're gone, I need you to promise you'll tell me everything and how you know so much."

He snarled down at her with his crisp blue eyes, his strong jaw pulsing under that short dark beard.

Her fingertips tingled with the urge to pet him.

*Not the time!*

"It's either that," she added, "or you can deal with the police, who will insist on taking Louie to a hospital." Not good because she suspected his issues stemmed from supernatural causes related to this man.

With a grunt, Távas nodded. "Very well. I agree."

Two minutes later, Forgetty had the police filing out of the room, believing they'd lost their way to another call involving a panty raid.

"That's right," she said in Portuguese, ushering them out. "The thieves have been hitting all the rooms. You must go door-to-door and ask all the guests if they're missing panties." She locked the door behind them.

With a whoosh, she closed her eyes and drew a breath. *That should keep them busy.* "Okay, they're gone, Távas. Now it's time for you to tell me what's going o—"

The stillness in the room jarred her. Wondering where Távas had gone, she walked to the bedroom, where Louie lay on his back, out cold. Távas sat beside Louie, holding his hand with a lost look in his eyes.

*A father's pain.* She'd seen the look hundreds of thousands of times in the eyes of parents. Wars, famine, natural disasters—the pain of losing a child was the sort of thing a human did not easily move past on their own. It was her most difficult duty as a deity, but she was always there, ready to ease their sorrow and help them heal. A very delicate procedure, but if done correctly at the correct time, it was possible to fade the pain of loss and leave behind the loving memories so that they might carry on. No, it didn't work with everyone, but like a surgeon, she'd learned that she could not save every patient.

"Távas, he's going to be okay," she whispered. She'd get to the bottom of this and free Louie from the poison in his soul. "But are you? Okay, I mean?"

He nodded slowly, his eyes stuck to Louie's peaceful face. The young man was quite beautiful, really. Dark features, high cheekbones, and wide lips.

"Funny, he doesn't look much like you," she said, though Távas was indeed beautiful—intense eyes, a strong jaw, and soft pillowy lips. She wouldn't describe him as exotic. More like fierce and classically male. *Not a wimpy feature on him.*

"He takes after his mother," Távas muttered.

*Távas is married?* Her soul twitched with regret. "Well, she is a lovely woman."

"Was. *Was* a lovely woman."

"Oh. I'm sorry."

"I hardly knew her," Távas said without emotion. "But I've spent the last few months searching for Louie." He turned his large frame and faced her. "I only found him three days ago."

"And I'm guessing the reunion hasn't gone so well."

"No. I am the sort of man no one would want as a father. Just as I am the sort of man no one would want as a husband."

The harsh bitterness in his voice sucked her in. Did this have something to do with Louie being infected?

She clasped her hands together and leaned her shoulder into the doorway. "So tell me, Mr. Liath, who are you?"

Távas looked at the floor for a moment and then slowly rose. "This is a conversation that requires tequila."

༄ ༄

With Louie passed out, Forgetty followed Távas into the dining area with the full panoramic view of Rio's coast, the night sky, and dark ocean. She hadn't noticed before, due to the commotion, but an entire meal had been laid out on the sleek black table in the dining area, just next to the living room.

Was that poached salmon stuffed with crab and filet mignon under those metal domes? It smelled delicious. *And thankfully cooked.*

Távas walked over to the bar in the corner and poured two small tumblers of golden liquid. He threw one back, repoured the glass, and then returned to her with both drinks in hand.

"You do drink, yes?" He held out the glass. "Because I plan on having at least four more, and I understand that drinking alone is an unacceptable practice by modern standards."

She took the tequila with a polite nod. "Modern standards are like underwear. People wear them for a while, then throw them out and get new ones." She lifted the glass. "Cheers."

He tapped the rim of his drink to hers. "And do you eat?"

"On occasion." *Every chance I get. I just don't want you to think I'm a gluttonous pig.*

"Excellent." He pulled out the chair closest to her and helped her slide in. "Because I'm starving." He walked around the table and sat to face her. Instead of speaking, his hard, troubled gaze moved to the plates of covered food on the table.

A melancholy silence filled the room.

"Listen, Mr. Liath—I mean, Távas. I think I can make this fairly simple. You tell me who you really are and how you know what I am. In return, I will tell you why I'm sitting here giving a crap."

He looked up at her with those penetrating eyes, the fleck of lavender seeming to sparkle. "And then what?"

She shrugged and took a small sip of the tequila. It was the good stuff, tasting of cinnamon and vanilla instead of the cactus gasoline she used for making margaritas. Yes, she knew her liquors since she often bartended at their nightclubs when her brother had been having too much fun to show up for work.

She set down the glass and met his unsettling gaze. "Why don't we leave the 'then whats' for after." Because honestly, she didn't know what came next. She couldn't see a future with Távas given his unchivalrous disposition, but she felt entirely intrigued by his contradictions.

*He's like a pit bull and a poodle packaged in the body of a god—metaphorically speaking.* She didn't find her brethren the least bit attractive. Not because they were siblings (because they weren't truly related by blood), but because they were physically perfect. She liked men with imperfections, character, and a few battle scars—the kind of beauty one could only achieve through living a life filled with mistakes, pain, and victories. The gods were flawless in appearance, making it impossible to ascertain the sort of life they'd led just from looking at them. *No, there are no stories to be told by our outer shells.*

Távas took a swig of his tequila and gave her a nod. "As you wish. We shall table our discussion until after dinner."

"No. I said we'd postpone talking about next steps until after we put our cards on the table, which starts now." She leaned back in her chair. "Who are you?"

"I am Távas Liath—as you already know."

It dawned on her that Távas meant peacock in ancient Hebrew and Liath was Gaelic for gray. *Very befitting.* "Thank you for repeating your name. Now tell me who you really are."

"Who do you think I am?"

She cocked her head. "You want to play coy? I just saved your son's life and then brainwashed a bunch of policemen for you."

"I am merely curious to know what sort of creature you think I am." He grinned slyly, exposing two sets of fine wrinkles in the corners of his eyes.

Her heartrate ticked up a bit. She was a sucker for that kind of stuff. It hinted at a man's maturity and character. *Though, he doesn't look a day over thirty-three.* His aura, on the other hand? Its blue ribbons screamed old soul.

"If I knew what you were," she began, rising from her seat, "I wouldn't be asking. But I don't have a moment to lose, so if you're not interested in coming clean, then it's time for me to lea—"

"I am a man. A plain old regular man."

She lowered herself again. "If you're just a man, then how do you know who I am?"

He stared into his glass, circling his fingertip around the lip. "I've met your sister Cimil."

*I should've known.* "You're one of her little minions, aren't you?"

"Do I look like a minion?" he scoffed.

"No. You're entirely too tall, but she put you up to this, right? What's in it for you? A ride on Minky? Free parking for life?"

"What's a Minky?" he asked.

"Answer the question."

"I am not working for Cimil, nor would I ever. I have simply met her."

"And from that you were able to figure out what I am?" *Not likely.*

"She went into a catatonic state, babbling about Twinkies, unicorns, demonic clowns and her sister 'Whatserface'—a goddess no one remembers who wears her gift like a curse."

"What's that supposed to mean?" she asked.

"After meeting you? My guess is that what was once a prison is now a shield. If given the chance to let the world see you, truly see you, you would still hide because you believe you're not worth seeing."

Forgetty stared into his eyes, fighting the urge to slap him silly. How dare he, a Neanderthal poster child, judge her like that?

"When did you figure out she and I were sisters?"

"The moment I saw you—your eyes, really. I've never seen that shade of turquoise on anyone except her."

"When did you first see me?" she asked.

"When my staff showed me your demo video before I booked you for the tour."

She sensed he was lying. The aura often shifted to a darker hue when one tried to hide something.

"Well," she said, "if you know who I am, then you know why I cannot believe you."

"No."

"Because," she drew a breath, "I am the Goddess

of Forgetfulness. No mortal has ever managed to truly remember me for more than five seconds."

He tilted his head. "Then how do you manage to have millions of followers?"

"Because they don't really remember me—it's more of a craving or dull sensation given off by my music, which triggers an awareness in their souls. But I could walk right by any one of them and they'd never know who I was."

"Sounds very lonely," he said, his voice deep and smug.

*Wrong response.* "No. Sounds like you're playing games." She rose from her seat and planted her hands on the table. "Why do you remember me?"

Calm and cool, Távas leaned back. "You tell me. You're the goddess. Because I assure you, I am human—born with a mother and a father like every other person on this planet."

Either he was a phenomenal liar or he was telling the truth because his aura hadn't flickered that time.

She mulled it over. She supposed if he were in fact born human, that could still leave werewolf—*or were-penguin*—and vampire as species options, but she would know. Those creatures had very distinct scents and energies. Távas had neither.

She let out a sigh and sank into her chair. "Well, the only explanation I can come up with is because the Universe chose you to be my mate."

"Your what?"

She groaned and pressed the heels of her hands into her eyes. "My mate. My one and only. I don't really believe in all that one-true-love, mate bull crap, but clearly there's something different about you if you're able to remember me when no one else can. You're immune to the effects of my energy, and the only reason I can think of for this is that you were chosen by the Universe for me." *How nauseating.*

He snickered, clearly amused.

"What's so funny?" she snapped.

"I knew you were hitting on me."

She frowned. "No. Ugh. And stash that bloated ego of yours. I think you're completely horrible and rude."

"Yet you kissed me, and we both know you liked it. Also, according to you—a divine being— the cosmos has chosen me to be your one true love." He chuckled to himself and threw back his drink. "Ironic."

"I said that *might* be why you remember me, but obviously I don't know for sure. I mean, look at you. Other than your tight ass, big arms and what I guess to be a washboard stomach underneath that shirt, you have zero appeal to me."

"My cock is huge. Don't forget that."

"Pfft. Is it as big as your ego? Because then I'd be impressed."

"It's big enough."

"Whatever." She got up and stepped away from

the table, feeling like she'd gotten absolutely nowhere with this man.

"Where are you going?"

She gave him a look, wanting to throttle him. Mostly because he'd let her down. A tiny part of her had hoped he'd come clean and tell her he was really a nice guy—one who deserved her love, but that for some reason, he had to pretend to be this complete asshole. That hadn't happened.

"Truth?" she said. "I'm going to go to my room, pack my things, and book a flight to LA, where my sister is hopefully throwing me a speed-dating party."

He bobbed his head. "Sounds…interesting?"

"Given the influence I have on pilots, you have no idea." In fact, she needed to call Acan and make sure he was on standby to help the plane land safely. *Seriously, if we get through this, I'm so getting my commercial pilot's license.*

He stood, moving to show her out as she made her way to the front door.

"Then I bid you safe travels, goddess." He opened the door.

She turned to face him one last time. "And I wish you luck with your son, because clearly he needs a father, and you are not suited to be one." He'd admitted it himself, which was why she'd be bringing Louie up to Cimil as soon as she got back to LA. They needed to help the young man, and quickly.

Suddenly, Távas had her by the throat and slammed her against the wall beside the door. Rage poured from his eyes. "How dare you."

His grip was firm and his hands rough, but with his strength, she suspected that if he'd wanted, he could've crushed her throat. Instead, his hand held her to the wall like a cage around her neck, allowing her to breathe.

"Let go of me, Mr. Liath, or I will punish you with the most excruciating pain you've ever known." One pulse of her light, and he'd be flying across the room.

"There is no pain you can inflict upon me worse than what I already have." His blue eyes flickered to coal-mine black.

*Ohmygods. It's inside him, too.* The same darkness that afflicted Louie afflicted Távas. It coated his heart and soul like tar.

*What is that?* she wondered. And how come she hadn't seen it until now?

Then it dawned on her. Before the Maaskab's downfall, they'd enslaved thousands of people, including some members of the gods' human army known as the Uchben. They would capture their soldiers, inject their veins with black jade, and then flood them with dark energy. The jade would absorb the toxins and allow the Maaskab to control the humans to do their evil bidding.

The only known cure was to take the humans to the realm of the gods, where the dark energy could be pushed out and replaced with divine light. This also meant the individual ended up an immortal demigod, a very, very big deal in their world. Only the most deserving of souls were given such an honor—the leaders of the Uchben, the most noble of humans, the strongest of the good vampires, and really, really good disco dancers (also known as Cimil's Law). In the gods' entire history, only one exception had been made, and that was Tommaso. He'd been one of their best soldiers but had been captured by the Maaskab. He'd committed heinous acts, including capturing one of her brothers' mates for a ritualistic sacrifice. In the end, Tommaso was apprehended and clemency was granted because her brother's mate forgave him and pleaded for his life. She argued that Tommaso had not been in control of his actions, though the gods saw it as a form of weakness. Had he been stronger, faster, smarter, he never would've ended up a Maaskab slave.

*Horseshit.* At one time or another, every one of the fourteen gods had lost to the Maaskab. Hell, once the evil priests had even managed to capture nearly all of them in a cenote—the freshwater pools they used as portals between worlds. Nevertheless, the other gods showed little mercy for anyone touched by the Maaskab, which meant they would never grant demigod status to someone like Louie or Távas. *Unless…*

She looked up at Távas. "Tell me, Mr. Liath, who you were before the priests got their hands on you and filled you with poison."

He dropped his hand. "I know not what you speak."

*Bullshit.* "It's now or never. Tell me what you can because my days are numbered unless I find *the one.*"

"What are you talking about?" he questioned, seemingly unconcerned.

"The same darkness that consumes you will consume me unless I find a mate."

His eyes flickered with suspicion. "Sounds ominous."

Was this a game to him? "It is. And if you care for your son, even a little, you'll answer my question."

"What exactly are you asking again?" he questioned. "Because I don't know of any priests, and I've certainly not been poisoned by anyone."

*Hmm…*Her bullshit meter had not gone off. On the other hand, she could now see the malevolent energy veined through his aura, and when all was said and done, what she really needed to know was if she could make the case to save him—to make him a demigod. If he had once been a good, good person who ended up this way against his will, she might be able to convince her brethren to help him. Especially given her circumstances.

She pushed away his hands and cleared her throat. "The question is: Why should someone like me love someone like you?"

"What makes you think I wish to have your love or ever give mine?"

"Godsdammit!" She shoved her hands at his chest, launching him to the floor, where he landed on his back. "This isn't a game, Távas. Give me a reason to believe you are worth saving. Make me understand why you of all people have been chosen to wake beside me every day for the rest of my existence. There must've been something special, something worthy about you before this *thing* happened to you."

Sizzling with anger, he quickly got to his feet and charged at her, putting them nose to nose. "I am not a good man. I never have been. I never will be."

"But do you want to be? Give me something!"

He stared into her eyes for a long moment before shaking his head no.

*Dammit.* She couldn't accept this defeat, and frankly something wasn't adding up. He claimed to be rotten to the core, but no one was born evil. Okay, except maybe Cimil, though even she had some goodness in her. Even she fought to be better. *When she's not too busy torturing people and messing with the planet's fate.* In any case, it just didn't make sense that the Universe would choose a bad man for her, one who was impossible to save because he had zero goodness inside him.

*No, there must be something redeeming about him.* Perhaps what he needed was motivation to come clean. *His son. He cares about his son.*

"Tell me, Távas," she said, "why did you go looking for Louie?"

He rubbed his scruffy chin, hesitating. "To kill him."

She jerked back her head. "What?"

"After I learned I had a son, my only thought was to find him and extinguish his soul."

*Holy crap. That is pretty evil.*

*Wait. No. Be hopeful, Getty.* Perhaps he had a good reason. "Did you want to kill him because you feared he'd be like you?"

"Yes."

*Awesome. He wanted to kill his son for the greater good! And I can't believe I'm cheering this.* "Well, you can't be all bad because, as messed up as killing your son would've been, you wanted to save the world from more men like you."

He shook his head and frowned. "No. I just hate competition."

*Dammit! No! That is so, so evil.*

"Oh gods." She rubbed her forehead. "We're all fucked."

"But…" he hesitated, "then I saw him."

"And?" Her heart accelerated, filling with a sprig of hope.

"And all I could think of was saving him."

"Saving him from being like you?"

He nodded, and she released a slow sigh of relief. It wasn't much to work with, but it was something.

"Why are you smiling?" he asked.

She ran her hands over the top of her head. "Because maybe it's not too late for you, which means it's not too late for me."

He grabbed her by the shoulders. "Goddess, let me make something perfectly clear. I am not your 'one.' I will never be good, nor do I wish to be."

She blinked up at him. "There is goodness in you even if you don't want it. You'd do anything to shield Louie from following in your footsteps, and you made an effort to make me feel special tonight."

"He's just a kid." He huffed. "And I wanted to get in your pants."

She smiled softly. "Okay."

"Okay what?"

"Okay. I'll let you in my pants." If he truly was her mate, his soul would start pulling hers away from the edge of darkness and she would do the same for him. Love was the most powerful force in the Universe, and more of it could only help him. From there, all she needed to do was prove to her brethren that he would not become a threat if made into a demigod, an act that could cure but not change one's true nature. It was the reason they were so strict about handing out the turquoise eyes. No one wanted to make the mistake of granting immortality to a jerkwad psycho.

"Well? Are we going to get frisky or not?" *Jeez, way to be romantic, Forgetty.*

Távas stared for a long, long moment, the air filled with static.

Suddenly, his soft lips slammed into hers. He poured himself into the kiss, and she felt his armor melt away, exposing his darkness, his regret, his surrender to the life he'd been handed and to the bad things he'd done.

*Wow.* He was, without question, evil. But in this moment, she also felt his soul reaching through hers, searching for the light.

Her heart swelled with hope. She could help him forget his past and start anew as a good man. *Yes, this is going to work.*

She reached to the sides of his scruffy jaw and held him tight to her mouth, inhaling his scent, his lust, and his darkness.

"What are you doing to me?" he panted.

She reached for his tie, ripping at the knot before tearing at the buttons on his shirt.

He took the cue and clawed at her dress until she was completely naked save her heels.

"Dear gods," he groaned. "You're hot enough to turn the blackest soul to gray."

She quirked a brow. "Uh, thanks?"

He grabbed her forcefully and pulled her close, snaking his muscled arms around her back, deepening the kiss.

She leaned into his tall frame, enjoying the hardness of his strong body and the heat of his skin seeping into her. Their mouths danced, greedily drinking in each other's kisses. She loved the way his pillowy lips moved and slid against hers. He wasn't afraid or intimidated by her, and he knew how to kiss.

Still dressed, he scooped her naked body into his arms and carried her off to the master bedroom. Her body felt too hot, too lost in him to notice what the room looked like. Some brown furniture, white carpet—who cared?

He put her down in front of a long dresser, turned her to face it, and shoved her forward. All she could think of was how much she needed to experience him—deep inside, touching her skin, breathing hard. In a moment's notice he had gone from abrasive lug to an exotic dish she needed to taste. Good or bad, he was an unknown flavor she craved.

*He's like evil brownies.*

She heard the zipper of his black slacks opening and the whoosh of fabric falling to the soft carpet before he let out a deep groan.

"I could look at that view all night." He gave her ass a slap, jolting her body upright.

"Hey." She looked over her shoulder. "What was that?"

"I'm evil. Remember?" He turned her back around, and before she could respond, he had his fingers between her soft folds, massaging her gently.

She gasped from the pleasant sensation. She couldn't remember the last time she'd been with a man.

*Try never. Never, ever, ever—*

"You're already wet for me," he said, sounding pleased, dipping his fingers into her entrance.

Her mind spun in a dizzy cloud of sexual need. Clearly, they had chemistry, despite his lack of compassion or kindness—something she hoped to remedy.

"Great observation," she panted. "Are you going to fuck me now?"

He removed his hand, and she quickly felt the head of his cock prodding at her entrance.

She braced her hands on the edge of the dresser, sticking her ass up in anticipation of a thorough pounding.

A moment passed. Then another.

"What are you waiting—" She turned her head, only to find him standing there with his shaft in his hand.

*Damn, that thing really is huge.* But it was the look of concern in his eyes, which were glued to her rear, that really caught her attention.

"What's the matter?" Because it certainly couldn't be her body. This goddess came equipped with forever-smooth skin, toned thighs, long legs and the kind of tits that were so perky and full that she never required a bra. The girls just did their thing all on their own. Not that she really knew what to do with all of that fine equipment, given relationships weren't ever on the menu. *It's like the Universe gave me a Ferrari I never get to drive.*

"Uh…" He suddenly bent down and slid on his pants.

*What the...?* Forgetty stood upright and turned to face him. "What the hell do you think you're doing?"

"This isn't happening." He zipped up his fly.

"Wow. You really are an epic evil asshole."

"You're right. Smart of you to notice." With torment in his hard, sinfully sexy eyes, he turned to leave the room.

She rushed around him, blocking his path. "Hey. You're not exactly my first choice either, unless we're counting your tall manly body and broad shoulders, but I'm almost out of time."

He crossed his arms over his chest. "And?" His blue eyes moved to her bare breasts.

"See. Right there. We have chemistry."

"Do we now?"

"Yes. And I think if we start there—knowing we're compatible in the bedroom—then it's the spark you need, the way forward for you and for us. Not to mention Louie."

He gave her the most peculiar look, somewhere between a frown and look of longing. It ignited a longing of her own. She wanted to help him. She felt his sorrow.

"I have no interest in changing," he spat, "or moving forward, or...*sparking*."

"Távas, I know you don't mean that. It's the poison inside you talking, and though you won't tell me how it got there, I have a solution to remove it."

"Beg." He crossed his thick, menacing arms over his broad chest.

"Sorry?" She blinked at him.

"You want me to fuck you, then beg."

"Uh!" Her mouth fell open. "I will *not* beg, you evil fuck."

"Then no evil fuck for you." He pushed past her, but she quickly caught up again. She couldn't believe he was doing this to her. Most of all, she couldn't believe she was actually considering begging.

*Damn you, Universe!* Her hardwiring to serve humanity really sucked eggs. Otherwise, she would walk right out that door and never look back.

"Why are you doing this to me, Távas?"

"Because, as I've told you, I am not a good man. Never have been, never will be, never want to be."

*Lies. All lies.* Only minutes ago she'd felt his soul clawing for the light, seeking salvation.

She held her hands up in surrender. "Fine. I get it. You're horrible, cruel, and unsalvageable. Now will you fuck me?" Because if her instincts were correct, if they bonded, his need to be something better would become stronger.

"Beg, goddess." He lowered his head, placing them nose to nose.

She swallowed down a lump of disdain. *He's got me by the short hairs and he knows it.*

She batted her eyelashes and smiled bitterly. "Please, mighty Távas, please bend me over that dresser and fuck me."

He studied her for a long moment, a cruel glint in his eyes. "Beg again. This time on your knees."

# CHAPTER TWELVE

"I can't believe this!" Cimil stomped her bare foot on the muddy jungle floor. "My piggy bank is gone."

"Are you certain?" asked Roberto, still in his black boxers, his bare chest on full display.

"Yes, I'm certain." She pointed to the clearing. "It was right there. And put away those pecs—I can't think straight when you show me your manly chest. Just makes me want to get out the peanut butter." All that mocha skin reminded her of milk chocolate, which reminded her of peanut butter cups. Of course, once that started, she couldn't stop herself from licking him from head to toe, and there was no time for that right now. They'd already lost two hours going at it like bunnies before even getting here.

"As you wish." He grabbed two large leaves from a nearby banana tree and held them over his nipples. "Better?"

"No. Now you're making me think of those delicious tamales." The kind that are wrapped in banana leaves and stuffed with all sorts of savory goodies. "Wait. Why can't I stop thinking about food?"

A long, long moment of silence filled the air.

Cimil gasped and covered her mouth.

Roberto dropped the leaves. "Oh, my sour little pickle, do not toy with me."

"I'm pregnant." She slid her hand over her stomach, immediately feeling that something wasn't right. "Oh goodness."

"Cimil, what's the matter?" He rushed to her side. "I know it happened quickly—like, in the last hour—but I thought you wanted another litter. You've been begging me for months."

"I do." She shook her head from side to side. "That's not the problem. I feel their lights. I feel…" She looked up at him, swallowing down her dread. "Their goodness."

It took a moment for Roberto to put the pieces together. "Uh-oh." His coco skin turned a sad shade of taupe.

"No shit, uh-oh! What kind of rotten swimmers did you give me, Roberto?"

"I don't know," he griped. "I'm a vampire. A very, very old one. Maybe my nut sack is past its expiration date."

She rolled her eyes. *Ugh. Vampires.*

He bellied up to her and pulled her close. "Cimil, do not fear. We will work this out. Together."

"But what can we do? The Universe will not stay in this state of chaos forever. And once all is set right again, the immortals who've flipped will return to their natural states. Our children, the ones who are currently malevolent little bastards, will be good, as they were meant to be. But these little suckers," she rubbed her stomach, "they will be supervillains once the world is right again." Cimil sighed.

Roberto placed his hand on her stomach. "Do not fret. Perhaps they will be grown by the time the Universe rights herself and they will already have mates to change their evil tendencies."

"It doesn't work like that; a mate only provides stability for one's soul so they can remain who they truly are. If you are a good soul, you are good. If you are evil, you are evil. A mate doesn't change a being's moral compass." This was the reason they were scrambling to find mates for the most powerful of the immortals. During this time of plague, a mate kept a person grounded in their true nature, like a vaccine or an antidote. "Make no mistake, once this wave of turbulence has made its way through the Universe's system, everything will go back to normal and everyone will be who they were truly meant to be."

"I see your point." Sadness filled Roberto's dark brown eyes. "One day, this will all be over, and you will be forced to dispose of our malicious offspring."

"Yes, because as Goddess of the Underworld, it is my job to vanquish evil souls and take them away. Unless it's Wednesday, in which case we all just have lunch." Her eyes widened with fear. "Roberto,

I have to get my powers back. I have to find a way to change course."

He groaned. "Cimil, my bitter melon ball of love and destruction," he took her hand, "haven't you learned by now? Every time you meddle, bad things happen. Not that I don't enjoy the excitement of always being on the edge of obliteration, but you cannot believe that trying to alter destiny will have a happy outcome. Look at where we are now—the Universe thrown into a state of chaos from the last time you tried to *fix* things." He made little air quotes when saying the word *fix*.

She stomped her bare foot in the mud. "Don't you dare blame me for this. I did what was needed in order to avoid the last apocalypse and save the entire planet from becoming slaves to evil vampires and the Maaskab."

"Yes, but you were the one who assisted them in the first place."

"Only because I was trying to fix the last problem I'd cause because I'd—oh, sauerkraut. Fine. I make a mess of things. But what are you suggesting I do now? Just let my children be born little angels so they end up the most wicked beings ever to roam the earth?"

"Perhaps you simply allow fate to run its course."

"Fate is a giant pig whore. She can suck it," Cimil snarled.

"I do not mean your sister Fate. I mean the

force of destiny intertwined within us all."

"No. I can't take the risk that things will simply work out. That faith bullshit is for humans and pussies. I'm a god. I was created by the Universe specifically to meddle. Proof being that she gave me powers." She drew a breath. "I have to try, Roberto. I must."

He took her hand and kissed the top. "Then what do you propose?"

"For starters, I need to get my powers back, but now that'll be impossible since someone has stolen my piggy bank. Which leaves only one option."

"Please do not tell me it involves clowns. I'm still recovering from the last botched clown world rescue."

That hadn't gone well. All that juggling.

She shivered. "No. I'm thinking that if I can't blackmail my brethren into returning my powers, then I will have to scare them into doing so." She grinned. "We'll have to create a situation so horrific, so shockingly ugly that they will have no choice but to beg for my assistance."

"You want to bring back disco, don't you? I knew there was a reason you keep petitioning for John Travolta's immortality."

"No. I want to bring back the Maaskab army."

He gave her a stern look. "Nooo, Cimil. That is far too risky. The Maaskab are too powerful when they have numbers on their side, and we are no match for any of them. We got lucky the last time they tried to take over."

True. The Maaskab had teamed up with evil vampires, drinking their blood, which gave them physical powers beyond any deity's, including the ability to sift. Their big mistake had been only taking blood from Roberto's evil vampire brother. With his brother's death, that entire bloodline perished. The Maaskab wouldn't be so foolish this time around.

"Well." Cimil threw her arms around Roberto's neck, the moonlight dancing through the trees on his black hair. She loved looking at him. She also loved that she could always count on him to do her bidding. "Then I suppose we'll just have to ensure all of the Maaskab are killed after I get my powers back." And, more importantly, before the Universe righted herself again. For the time being, however, the Maaskab were the nicest people on the planet. Her nanny included.

*Such a shame he won't stay good forever. He bakes the best cookies and the kids just adore storytime.* He really knew how to scare the hell out of them with tales from his good old days—ripping out virgins' hearts, plucking out people's eyeballs—all sorts of squishy fun!

"Let's get back home," she said. "Oh, and since I'll be busy rounding up the remaining Maaskab and finding new recruits for their army today, I'll need your help setting up Forgetty's speed-dating party—we still have her little *sitch* to deal with." Of course, if Cimil got her powers back, she would hopefully find a way to maneuver around all this.

*Of course, if I fail…kablewy!*

"I'd almost forgotten about your sister." Roberto ran his hands through his long black hair and then scratched his scruffy beard. "Listen, cupcake, I would love to assist, but I know nothing about matchmaking. Perhaps I should deal with the Maaskab instead."

"No. Let me deal with the Scabs. As for Forgetty, I've already put out feelers and compiled a list of eligible immortal men. You just have to screen the candidates." Cimil patted Roberto's cheek. "I'll be fine."

"Then let us get home. I'm sure the children will be waking soon, and we don't want them killing more neighbors."

"Right. Oh! And if you don't mind, can we make a quick stop? I have to free Minky from some fucking mermen."

Roberto's face contorted. "Ick. I hate mermen. They smell funny—like fish and expensive cologne."

"Well, they're about to smell like a Japanese dinner. 'Cause one look at you and they'll sushita themselves." Cimil snorted. "Get it. Because they smell like sushi…" Her voice faded off as she realized Roberto didn't laugh with her. "Oh, fuck off. That was funny. Let's go."

"Of course, but might I ask, what of Tula?"

"Dammit! I forgot about her, too. Well, she's on

her own now. I can't deal with my uterus dumplings, creating a Maaskab army, getting my powers back, speed dating for Forgetty, and saving Tula from Zac, and Zac from the mermen, all while looking fabulous for you and keeping the world in check. Sacrifices must be made, which means Tula will have to fend for herself."

"Do you think she will be all right?" Roberto asked.

Cimil shrugged. "What's the worst that could happen?"

❧ ❦

Zac and Tula crouched behind the shadow of a leafy bush, waiting for the coast to be clear on the dock.

"These mermen sure are a busy people," Tula noted.

In the last hour they'd watched them load and unload boats, carrying supplies inland. It was the middle of the night. Didn't they ever sleep?

"They're godsdamned annoying is what they are. We'll never get to my yacht like this."

"Zac?" Tula whispered, wrapping her soft hands around the crook of his arm. "I didn't know you knew how to sail a boat."

"Errr…" *Dang it.* He actually didn't. And if the poor captain hadn't been freed from the closet, he'd certainly be dead by now.

Zac's heart cramped with guilt. He couldn't

believe the horrible things he'd done, including killing the entire crew of that ship and five of the mermen he'd fought with. Not that Zac had an affinity for the cocky bastards, but it went against everything in his soul to kill unnecessarily. At least good people. *The bad ones, not so much.* When he got through this, he was going to make amends to the poor families of all the victims. He'd start with apologizing to Roen. Certainly a man such as himself, his entire culture once enslaved and forced to perform senseless killing, would understand why Zac had done such vile things.

*Or I may need to do them again if we are caught.* Though Zac hoped it wouldn't be the case, men born into warrior cultures understood that protecting one's mate stood above all else. And, certainly, Roen would understand how he'd been manipulated by Cimil. This entire situation had been her fault.

*And foolish me for ever listening to my sister.* When would he learn? *Once this is straightened out, I'm going to make sure Cimil pays and justice is served.* She'd lied to him every step of the way, telling him that Tula was not his mate.

*She is the love of my existence.* So much so that he would give up everything for her, including his desire. *Just as long as I have her in my life and by my side.* But that meant protecting her, keeping her pure heart intact so that she would always love him.

"I saw a rowboat down the shore, Tula. We will have to leave in that and make our way back to the mainland."

"I will go anywhere with you, Mr. Zac. As long as we are together."

He turned and looked at her sweet face glowing in the moonlight. "I won't ever leave you, my love. Not ever."

They made their way to the small rowboat and Zac helped her in.

ॐ ॐ

"Zac?" Two hours later, Tula shivered against Zac's body as the small wooden dinghy bobbed in the ocean. "I'm c-cold. So cold."

*Fucking hell. I did not think this through.* It was the dead of winter, the middle of the night, and the rough waters of the North Pacific was no place for a human in a cotton dress. A wet one at that. He'd just been so focused on escaping that he hadn't stopped to think of her safety. He'd never been someone's protector, never thought of anyone but himself, and now he realized just how unequipped he was for the job.

*I am. The worst. God. Ever.*

Zac pulled her closer, running his hand over her long wet hair. "I'm so sorry, Tula. I forgot how fragile you are."

"Wha-what are we go-going to do?" She shivered out her words, her warm breath creating puffs of steam in the moonlight.

If they hadn't already, it wouldn't be long before the mermen discovered that the two of them had escaped. Soon they'd send men on boats and in the water to hunt for them.

*Or rescue us.* At least Tula would be. He'd be tossed to the bottom of the ocean.

*I don't care.* "We must turn back, my love," he said, rubbing his hands on her shoulders. "Otherwise, you will freeze out here."

"Z-Z-Zac?"

"Yes, my love?"

"I can't feel my fingers."

His heart sank into the deep dark waters beneath them. He had nothing to offer her save the warmth of his own body, which wasn't enough.

He let her go and moved to the middle bench, taking the oars. He began rowing with brute strength. "Hang on, Tula. You just need to make it for another hour. Maybe two. The mermen are out there searching, and I will make sure they find us."

For thirty minutes, he pumped his arms, pushing the small vessel through the choppy waves. But with each stroke, he could see her lips turning bluer, her eyes closing. He could either row or try to keep her warm, buying her precious minutes, but he could not do both.

He ceased rowing.

"Why did you s-s-stop-p?" she muttered.

"Fuck, Tula." His eyes filled with tears as he came to her side and tried to keep her from going into hypothermia. "I'm a god. And this is the best I can do for you?" *This cannot be.*

"All I ever wanted was to f-fall in love w-with a man, w-with all my heart. You gave me th-that."

"And I love you, Tula. I truly do."

She slowly moved her head from side to side, the spray of waves hitting them in the face. "Then hold me. Make love to me. But d-don't let me die like thi-this."

He pulled her head into his chest. "Tula, I can't begin to tell you how much you've meant to me, how you've changed me. Not just as a god, but as a man. For the first time in seventy thousand years, I understand what love is, which only stings harder. Because in the moment when it matters most, when I would give anything to save you—my life, my eternal soul, my really awesome hair—I am helpless. I have nothing to give you but my love, yet it won't save you."

"It's e-e-nuff-f-f-er me."

In a million years or a million lifetimes, it would never be enough for him. But he couldn't fly. He couldn't magically produce a fire. All he could do was pray for help. *Please, Universe. I'm begging. Do not let her die. Take me instead.* He closed his eyes and tilted his face toward the heavens, praying for his voice to be heard, if not by the Universe, then by the gods. One of his brethren had to be in their realm right now. His brother K'ak or Akna, the Goddess of Fertility.

No one replied.

He released a gritty, bitter breath. What should he expect? It wasn't as if he'd led an exemplary life worthy of favors from the Universe. *Or anyone for that matter.* But this wasn't about him. It was about Tula, the first person to ever give him purpose in a way that was deeply personal. The rest was just work, his obligation.

He looked at her sweet face with delicate features, tiny icicles forming on her golden lashes.

*Fuck.* The light inside her was fading fast. She was dying. Fucking dying. How had he done this to her?

His soul cracked in two. There were no words for the suffering coursing through him, but even now, he could only think of her.

The waves calming, he stood in the rocky boat, with feet apart. He held out his hand.

She glanced up at him with fear in her eyes. "Wha-what are you doing?"

"Dance with me, Tula." The only thing he wanted to do was see her smile. *One last time.* "I never should've taken you from the island. I'm a fool, a stupid asshole, and now I'm doing the only thing I can to make the last few moments of our time together mean something beyond your physical suffering."

"My feet are frozen," she whimpered. "I can't stand."

With tears in his eyes, Zac scooped her into his

arms. "I will carry you, my love." *In my heart. Always.*

She buried her face in his neck. "I'm so cold, Zac."

"I know, my love." He swayed his body. "Just listen to my heartbeat." He tilted his head to the side, keeping his tears from her face as her heart slowed. After a few moments she drifted off to sleep, and he sat cradling her in his arms.

An hour passed, and another. Then her heart stopped dead.

Time stopped with it.

Suddenly, his existence flashed before his eyes, and his soul bucked with rage. He couldn't remember what it was like before her, and now there was no future. Not without her.

"I'm so sorry, my love," he whispered.

# CHAPTER THIRTEEN

With rage in her heart, Forgetty slowly sank to her knees in front of Távas, his harsh gaze of disapproval drilling down on her.

"That's right, goddess. Now beg," he snarled.

Her entire body—still naked—revolted, but she couldn't *not* do this one simple act of setting aside her ego. Too many lives were at stake, and for that reason, she could still hold her chin high.

"Please fuck me."

He scoffed with disdain.

*Wait. Why does he look pissed?* She was doing just as he asked.

It dawned on her that he was enjoying this act of humiliation and submission even less than she. And was it her imagination, or was his aura turning darker by the minute? In fact, when she'd met him, his aura had been blue—a little somber, but good. Now it was dark gray with swirls of blue.

But why? What could cause him to give in to the poisons inside him?

Knowing that the window was closing fast, not only for him, but for her as well, she focused her attention on the matters at hand.

*I have to try to make a connection with him.* Otherwise, they'd both be lost. She could feel the malevolent energy invading her cells one by one, like a cancer.

She reached for the fly of his black slacks, but he caught her hand. "Why are you allowing me to treat you like this?"

"What does it matter?" she asked. "I'm begging like you asked. Now give me what I want."

"Don't be so pathetic," he growled. "Reject me, goddammit. Walk away. Tell me to go fuck myself."

She blinked up at him. He had purposely been trying to offend her? "First you take me in that room and chicken out at the last moment. Then you ask me to beg, so I do. Now you want me to leave. What is going on, Távas? What aren't you telling me?"

He marched into the bedroom, returning with her clothes in a crumpled wad. "Go. Now."

She got to her feet, and he shoved the pile at her chest.

"Not until you come clean," she said. "Why did you hire me? Why did you ask me out? And why are you now trying to push me away? Something is happening to you—I can see it."

"Why are you standing naked in front of me like some pathetic, weak whore?"

"Whoa." She resisted the urge to slap him or castrate him or hurt him in some way worthy of such an insult. "Nice try, but it won't work, Távas.

I'm not leaving until you tell me the truth."

"The truth is I thought I might like to bed you—you look like you might be a nice fuck. But in the short amount of time I've gotten to know you, the real you, I realize I could never want such a sad, lonely woman. Plus, you're really skinny and in need of a tan. I like my women with meat and pigmentation."

*Ouch.* "And the note with flowers, saying sorry? What was that for?"

"I never sent you any flowers."

"Liar."

He opened the door. "Out."

"Remember when I told you that I needed to find a mate? Well, it's a matter of life or death for billions of people."

"And?"

"You're my best chance to prevent my soul from turning evil and wreaking havoc on every living being on this planet."

"Not my problem." He pointed out the door.

"Oh, yes. It is because…" Like a rubber band breaking, Forgetty felt every molecule in her soul snap. "Oh, shit." She doubled over in pain, a burning sensation coursing through her veins.

Távas stared down at her. "What is happening?"

"Run, Távas. Take Louie and run…" She groaned out her words.

He bent to help her up. "What is the matter with you?"

"Fucking moron! Go! Get out of here."

"I am not leaving."

*Now he wants to play nice? Now?*

But those thoughts of selflessness would be her last. The light and goodness inside extinguished with a sputter. And like a switch had been flipped, she felt her body let go of the need to do right. All she could think of was how to inflict the most possible pain on everyone and everything.

She reached out her hand and grabbed Távas's arm, opening up the floodgates. He dropped to the floor unconscious.

"Let's see how good you are at begging."

⌘ ⌘

When Távas woke, it was to the worst headache he'd ever had, and his brain felt like overcooked noodles. He moved his arms, wanting to press his palms to the sides of his head, quickly realizing he had been duct taped to a chair in his room.

*What the fuck?* He jerked his wrists, feeling the tape bite into his flesh.

"Hiya, sweetheart." Now fully clothed in her little dress, the Goddess of Forgetfulness sat on his king-sized bed, scarfing down a plate of food.

"I see you're enjoying the dinner I ordered us."

She shoveled a giant forkful of salmon into her mouth. "Hmmm…" She rolled her eyes in ecstasy.

"I'm pleased you like it," he said. "Now untie

me."

She swallowed her food. "Nope. I have plans for you, Távas."

*Damn her.* Why had she not gone when he'd given her the chance? She had no idea what she'd gotten herself into, who he truly was: the most evil fucking bastard on the planet. There was no limit to the pain he could inflict on the masses, nor the horrific things he'd done, all to serve his need for power.

"Let me go, goddess, or you will regret it."

"I think not." She set her plate of unfinished food on the nightstand and scooted off the bed. "Because now that I've been unshackled from the restraints of my morality, I finally get to do anything and everything I've ever wanted. Starting with torturing the hell out of you." She plucked the steak knife from her plate, stood, and sauntered over. The criminal gleam in her eyes gave him cause for worry.

"Whatever you're thinking of doing, goddess, just remember that nothing in this world comes without a price."

She laughed into the air. "Shut your fucking piehole, Távas." She stepped forward and drove the knife right into his thigh.

"Ahhh! Sonofabitch. Why did you do that?" Not that he didn't deserve it, but hell! That hurt.

She wagged her finger at him. "Uh-uh-uhh… The question you should be asking is what it will take to keep me from doing it again."

"You do not frighten me." He moved to kick her, only to realize she'd taped his ankles, too.

"Perhaps I don't frighten you yet, but let me tell you how this is going to go." She stood directly in front of him, feet apart, knife balanced on the tip of her index finger.

*Impressive.* He liked a woman who could wield a steak knife.

She continued, "First, I'm going to ask you some questions, and you are going to answer. Every time you lie—and I'll know when you do—I will cut something off. Once I run out of interesting body parts to remove, I will go into the next room and get to work on Louie. And then, when I'm all done, and I have everything I want from you, I will unleash my powers. Everyone will forget who they are, where they came from, and any knowledge they've acquired since birth. Except for you, of course, because you're immune to me." She smiled wickedly. "It's gonna be fun."

Hell, normally he would be the first to agree, but things were different now.

"What do you want to know?" he asked.

"Who are you?"

"I've already told you that," he replied.

She shoved the knife forward, slicing into his calf.

"Ahh!" The warm blood dribbled from his leg.

"Oops. Looks like you've sprung a leaky-poo, Mr. Liath. Care to try that answer again?"

No. He did not. The more she knew, the worse for him. And he needed to protect Louie—from who he used to be, from who he could become again. *Damn, being good is exhausting.*

"Once more, Távas," she said. "Who are you?"

He had to lie. She couldn't know the truth. "If I tell you, will you let Louie go?"

"Nope. Besides, he's still got a few more hours to go before he wakes up, and I'm not carrying him off while I've got you by the nut sack." She looked up at the clock on the wall. "Sixty seconds. And give me the truth or the next jab will be in your crotch."

"You wouldn't dare."

In reply, she placed the tip of the blade right over the bulge in his pants.

She drove a hard bargain. "Fine. I, uh…I used to be in the record business—sales, specifically. I would like to claim that I was good at it, but I wasn't. Mostly because I got into drugs, which led to a few scams and finally kidnapping." The kidnapping part was true. He'd done plenty of that in his lifetime. Murder, too.

"Liar!" She raised the knife, aiming right for his sacred jewels.

"Gods! Okay! I'll tell you what you want to know."

"Oh, I know you will. But I told you I'd take a piece of you if you lied. I meant it." She strutted around him like a hungry cat, doing several laps. "I think I'll leave your cock for last. But let me see…

Perhaps an ear." She nicked his right lobe with the tip of the blade. He winced. "Or perhaps a cheek?" She made a small cut into the soft flesh.

"Goddess," he growled, "whatever point you're trying to make, you've made it. Put the knife away."

"Goddess? Don't you mean 'pathetic whore'— too skinny and pale to deserve your presence?"

He hadn't meant it. "I merely wanted you to leave."

"Oh," she chuckled, "I'm not leaving." She grabbed him by the hair and began sawing at the long strands.

*What the...* "Not the hair." He had worn it long since he was fifteen. It felt like a part of him.

"You're getting off lucky." She tickled his nose with the thick lock. "Now, what is it you were about to tell me?"

"I am not who I claim to be, as you suspected, but the reason I can't tell you is for the good of that young man in the other room."

She stared into his eyes. "You're telling me the truth."

He nodded.

"Then I suppose I should reward you." She took the knife, and he closed his eyes, expecting the reward to be another puncture wound.

He felt a dull pressure slide up his leg and then his thigh. He opened his eyes, only to see her cutting away at half his pants.

"Wait. No. Do not do that." He wanted her

more than she could ever comprehend, but if she fucked him, there'd be no turning back. It was the reason he'd tried to revolt her with his despicable behavior. Of course, his insatiable attraction got the best of him. Nevertheless, at the moment of truth when he was finally about to have the woman he'd wanted his entire life, he'd done the right thing. He'd pushed her away, knowing his lust couldn't be sated with one measly night. He'd dreamt of her and him and of a life together for far too long. *She doesn't understand what this is.*

"I've got the knife and a wicked streak, not to mention superpowers. I can do anything I like." She snickered.

"No, dammit. Do not do this, goddess." He struggled in the chair as she cut away half his pants, leaving him exposed on one side. On his upper half, he still wore his white shirt with the buttons torn off.

She smiled at him with those big turquoise eyes, her lips pursed. Dammit, she was so beautiful. The way her golden hair caught the light and the light made her skin shimmer as if dusted with magic. She'd taken his breath away the first time he'd seen her and every moment since then. But most of all, he'd seen something in her that was impossible to forget—the selfless love he once had before this never-ending nightmare began. Not that he was a victim—that had only been the case initially. Once the darkness took hold, he'd stopped struggling and embraced his place in the world. It was like Cimil had told him all those years ago. "You can never be good, Ta'as. Because what is good without evil? What is love with hate? What is life without death? It's all meaningless." Cimil could never get his name right, but her prediction had been correct. The moment he'd surrendered to his role, everything in the universe felt right. Still, there was always this small piece of him that longed to be good, to love, to open his eyes once more and truly see the beauty of a dawn.

The goddess was just like those first rays of sunlight—utterly breathtaking—which was why he'd struggled to keep his distance. But the goddess kept popping out of thin air and bumping into him. After the third time, he knew it was no mistake that the two of them collided repeatedly. *Just as we are doing now.* Because what she did not know was that they were two sides of the same coin. The Universe had been trying to stick them back together.

*Which is why we cannot fuck.*

She sat across his nearly naked lap and wrapped her arms around his neck. "Umm...you feel delicious, Mr. Liath."

He looked at her sinfully beautiful face and delicate lips, feeling his cock stir.

*Distract her.* "What is your name?"

Her eyes widened. "Sorry?"

"Your name? What is it?"

She gave her head a little shake from side to

side. "I don't have one."

"What? How do you not have a name?"

"What's the point in having a name when no one will remember it?"

"But they must call you something?"

"Forgetty, Getty, Whatsherface. On a good day, it's lady or ma'am. On a bad day it's hey you."

"Those are not names worthy of a beautiful goddess."

She tweaked his nose. "I think you are right."

"What name have you always liked?" he asked, hoping to distract her long enough to think of a solution besides sating his lust between her thighs.

"I'm not sure." She poked her chin with her index finger and looked up at the ceiling. "How about Kianto Lacandon?"

"Sounds like a cream for rashes. What does it mean?"

"Goddess of diseases. I think it has a ring."

"While it certainly captures your deadly nature, it fails to capture your timeless beauty."

She shrugged. "I suppose."

"Any other names?"

"I've always like Celine."

"Like the singer?" he asked.

"Who doesn't love her theme song for the *Titanic*?"

*Me.* "And you call yourself evil?"

"Good point. How about Gor?"

"God of Thunder?" he asked.

"No. Just short for gory."

He shook his head no.

"Pookie?" she suggested.

"Sounds like a fart."

"Oh, I know: Fuji, like the mountain. That's powerful and magnificent."

"Reminds me of an apple, though I do admit, you've nailed the whole temptation and sin thing, so an apple-esque name isn't out of the question."

She stared deeply into his eyes. "Then why did you reject me?" she whispered.

Every cell of his being fought to lie, but just like he hadn't been able to deny his attraction or keep away from her, he felt himself quickly giving in to his need to please her. It was like those stupid flowers. He'd wanted her to feel loved, but knew it could never be him, thus the note saying sorry.

"Oh, feels like someone's changed his mind about that rejection," she purred.

*Likely the effect of her sitting on my nearly naked cock.* The heat of her entrance pulsed through the fabric of his torn pants and her dress. *I'm going to lose this battle, aren't I?*

He sighed in defeat, the pull to submit to her overwhelming. "You're too beautiful, goddess. Too perfect. Too everything I've ever wanted and do not deserve. That is the truth."

They locked eyes for several long breaths, and then she leaned forward and planted a soft kiss on his lips.

The impact was instantaneous. Her warmth rushed through his body. He inhaled her scent, wanting to commit every floral note to memory. It was only a question of moments before he fully gave in to her.

"Aurora," he whispered. "Goddess of the sunrise, of a light consisting of natural, unfailing beauty that has managed to capture man's attention since the first human walked the earth."

She stared into his eyes, showing him that light, and he knew he was lost.

Her eyes teared as her soft pink lips curled into a gentle smile. "Aurora. I like it."

"Let me go now."

Her turquoise eyes narrowed. "Why?"

"Just promise you'll take Louie far, far away from me," he whispered. "Cure him. Show him how to be good."

"What do you mean?" She spoke softly.

"I am the Maaskab king, Aurora. I have been for over two thousand years. And my vacation is over."

She jerked her head back. "I-I don't understand."

"What is there to understand? I've tried to resist you. I thought I could sate my needs by bedding you and still walk away. But that thin thread I've been hanging by has now snapped."

She covered her mouth as her mind put all of the pieces together.

*Yes, goddess. Connect the dots.* He was a man so

powerful that even the gods feared him. He'd once taken her brother Chaam and turned him into his puppet. He had once subdued nearly the entire population of vampires and made them his slaves. He'd even captured the gods, tormented them for decades, and made their lives a living hell, all for his entertainment. Of course, they could not die, so they eventually wiggled out of his trap, but no one could dispute the fact that he was the most evil, sadistic, cutthroat bastard on the planet.

*At least I was until four months ago.*

"You flipped," she said, rising from his lap and going to sit on the edge of the bed to face him, her expression somewhere between sickened and fear. "You've been trying to keep us from bonding so you wouldn't fall in love and turn back to your old evil self."

He nodded. "Very smart." The sudden change had happened when he'd come across a crazy woman named Charlotte, who happened to be mated to one of his disciples, Tommaso. She'd come to their encampment in search of Tommaso, only to become their prisoner. It was then that she told Távas about the plague sweeping through the immortal community. Perhaps it was she who'd brought it to their camp. In either case, she knew exactly which buttons to push in order to trigger his change from monster to man.

"After my transition," he said, "I spent the first few weeks wandering the jungles of Southern

Mexico near our camp, unsure of what had happened to me. Every sin, every cruel act I'd ever committed came back to haunt me—the result of growing a conscience, I suppose. However, being a pragmatic man, I knew I could not be the only Maaskab suffering with this affliction. So I used my gifts to seek out my toughest soldier, who'd gone AWOL months earlier: Cimil's nanny. I can't begin to tell you how strange it was to see my most giftedly cruel soldier of the dark arts, who I trained with my own two hands, lovingly holding one of Cimil's babies.

"But it was then that I remembered Louie's mother. Seventeen years ago, she had been just another human we'd intended to use for sacrifice. But something about her, something deep inside her soul spoke to mine. We became attached to one another, and I set her free. I told my men that she'd escaped, but not before she and I made love. A year later, one of my men came to me with her head in a box—a gift he'd thought would please me. 'There is a child, but I saved it for the full moon next week,' he'd said."

"What did you do?" Aurora asked, her pale face filled with anguish.

"After I slaughtered ten of my men—the ones involved in killing Louie's mother—Cimil appeared. I had met her many times over the centuries, so it was no surprise when she showed up to escort my men's souls to wherever she takes bad people. But this time, I asked her to take Louie, too. 'Far, far away from me. Somewhere I will never find him,' I'd said. She agreed in exchange for one thing."

"What?" Aurora asked.

"She knew that you and I would meet some day—a premonition, I suppose—and she made me promise that I would not pursue you."

"Oh gods. I should've known." She balled her fists. "All this time, Cimil knew about you."

"Yes. But it doesn't matter, goddess. Deal or no deal, there is no future for us. Cimil knows that. I know that. And when I turned good and asked her to help me find Louie a few months ago, she said she didn't know where he was but that she'd help me search for him if I helped you. She said you needed a break, that things hadn't been so easy for you lately."

"The rave tour was her idea?"

"It was all for you." And, frankly, he'd been eager to be close to this beautiful goddess, even if it meant keeping her at arm's length.

"So Cimil made you promise not to get involved with me, but then made you help me?" she asked.

"Typical, sadistic Cimil. However, one look at you, and I knew it would be impossible to stay away. You must believe me when I say, Aurora, that you are so much more than you know, even if mortals do not remember you." He drew a slow breath and let it go with a sigh. "You matter even if the world doesn't know you exist, just as you told Louie tonight."

Yes, he'd been listening to her every word, and it had been his downfall now that he thought about it. Because from that moment on, he was in serious jeopardy of falling in love. She understood something that had taken him a thousand years to comprehend: we all had a place. We all mattered. *Like a pebble matters to the ripples on a pond. Like a single note matters to a song.*

"I have to go," she said.

Still taped to the goddamned chair, he struggled to free himself. She needed to accept the truth. "Aurora—"

"Don't call me that! I am the nameless one. The Goddess of Forgetfulness. And you are wrong; I am nobody."

"You are my light. And it is already done."

"What? What's done?" she asked.

"You opened your heart to me, to the possibility of me, the first time we kissed. It is I who has resisted our bond." He gave her a stern look. "I'm no longer resisting."

"No. No. I don't believe y—"

He felt the darkness flood his veins and, with it, two millennia of power. The kind a god should fear. "Welcome back to your true self, Aurora. Now it is you who should run. And take Louie with you."

# CHAPTER FOURTEEN

Life was crazy. But her life was fucking chaos. *How can this be possible?*

Forgetty threw her huge yellow suitcase onto her bed, thankful for the familiar comforts of her LA penthouse, after her long, exhausting trip home. Honestly, she considered this big messy planet her home, but having a tiny space—decorated entirely in happy yellow and oranges—kept her spirits up.

*Especially now.* She still couldn't make sense of everything that had happened in Rio. The time in Távas's hotel room had been like a dream, then a nightmare, and then it was just a blur somewhere in between.

*The king of the Maaskab. Távas. My mate.* She was going to kick the crap out of Cimil! All this time she knew. All this time Cimil could have said something and helped her find a way through this. But no. Instead, her sister, a sister she'd been loyal to for over seventy thousand years, hid the truth. And manipulated Távas.

*There is no excuse.* Not when Cimil had used her gifts repeatedly for her own selfish agendas. *Or for making others suffer.* Which really was Cimil's favorite form of entertainment. But Cimil had had a million opportunities to intervene and give her a chance at happiness. *I could've even met Távas before he became a Maaskab.* Had she known—*ugh!*—things could've turned out differently from this fucking impossible mess.

Forgetty wrung her hands. *I'm going to kill her. And then I'm going to disown her. You've robbed the last person of their happiness, Cimil. The fucking last!*

A loud knock on her front door startled her. "Louie! Could you get that?" she called out.

Yes, she'd kept her promise to Távas, though she was unsure how she was going to remove the poison inside him if the gods refused to help.

"No. I'm still throwing up!" he called out from the bathroom. "Thank you very much."

*Teenagers. Always so dramatic.* "How many times do I have to say I'm sorry?"

"I'll let you know once my asshole isn't in my throat, spewing diarrhea."

She walked over to the guest bath and found him crouching over the porcelain god. Or goddess. "Language, son. Language."

"Don't call me son." He heaved.

She rolled her eyes and went for the door. One look in the peephole put a smile on her face.

"Belch!" She jerked open the door and threw her arms around him, immediately noting the lack of squishiness. She pulled away and looked him over. "Someone's been working out."

"Margarita is the only cocktail I need these days, so I go by Acan. Plus, I've started giving classes at her gym. Abs Like a God—that's what I call it. Seems to be a hit with all of the newly single dads."

Forgetty bobbed her head. "Sounds promising. Come in." She stepped aside and allowed him to pass. "So, what brings you here, and how did you even know I was back in town?"

Louie's loud retch grabbed his attention.

"Who's that?" he asked.

"That's Louie, my new son. He's still getting over the near plane crash we had this afternoon." She pointed at Acan. "Oh. I guess that's how you know I'm here."

"Yeah. Next time, don't wait until the plane is out of fuel to call me for landing assistance."

She crinkled her nose. "I kind of dozed off. A long flight. So what can I do ya for?"

Acan stared out the window, a look of emptiness in his eyes.

*Oh boy. Here we go.* "Acan? Belch? Dr. Decapitation?" She snapped her fingers. "Wakie, wakie."

"Oh." He jostled his head from side to side. "Sorry. I forgot why I was here."

*Shocking.*

"Dude, where am I?" Louie stumbled from the bathroom.

Acan looked at her. "Who's that?"

*He's already forgotten.*

"Louie. My adopted son. But never mind that.

Why are you here, again?"

"Ummm. Okay…" Acan scratched his head. "Oh, I know. Roberto asked me to help out at your party this weekend. A singles mixer?"

"Oh, crap. I completely forgot about that."

"You? You forgot?" he asked.

"It's been a long week," she explained.

"But you never forget."

"How would you know?" she replied. Acan never remembered anything specific about her or her life.

"Huh?"

"Never mind. The speed-dating party should be cancelled."

"Forgetty! You've found a mate?" Acan asked. "Who?"

*Oh, I so don't want to tell him.* Acan would think she was mad for even attempting to help Távas. The gods outright loathed the man. They'd sooner dismember their own bodies with a pair of tweezers than help the evil king.

"The relationship isn't exactly like what you have with Margarita," Forgetty explained. "My mate is…well, we can't be together. Not yet. But I'm hopeful there's a way."

"I don't understand."

"Neither do I." Because it turned out that she and Távas were opposite sides of the coin. If he was good, it was because he rejected her, which would make her bad. If she was good, it was because they had bonded, which would return him to his true evil self. And once this plague passed, nothing would change. She would be driven toward the light, and him away from it.

She sighed with despair. "It's a clusterfuck, brother. Like no other."

"What are you going to do?"

She didn't know. Especially if the gods turned down her request for help, which was ninety-nine point nine nine nine percent certain.

"I suppose I'll have to find someone more suitable, someone who won't just ground me now, but who will love me for the rest of my existence." As is, Távas was not that man. Though, at this moment, his love—from his evil-to-the-core heart—was the only thing preventing her from flipping and harming billions of people.

*It's kind of sweet, really. In an entirely wicked-Maaskab, evil-Mayan-priest kind of way.*

"So the singles mixer is still on?" Acan asked.

"No. I mean yes. I mean…I don't know." She didn't want to open her heart to the possibilities of another man. What she wanted was Távas, the good version, anyway. Yes, he lacked sophistication in the art of seduction, but so did she. And, yes, his heart was black from two millennia of torturing the gods and murdering humans, but she couldn't forget one key piece of information: his soul. Plague or not, it had reached out to her. It thirsted for her light. But because of his past, he refused to believe there was hope for him.

*If I could just figure out how to use my powers on him, he might forget all the things he's done and then see the light.*

She looked up at her brother's face. "Acan, is your mate, Margarita, immune to your powers?"

He blinked, giving it some thought. "When we were courting, my influence was minimal, but now that we've bonded, my power over her is immeasurable. She's hypersensitive to my energy and moods, and I am the same with her. Our souls are connected at the deepest level. She even gains weight when I drink alcohol. It's actually pretty funny."

Forgetty scratched her cheek. "So tell me how Távas can be my mate, but completely unaffected by me? I can't even make him forget my face." Everyone forgot her face.

Acan rubbed circles over his flat stomach, likely due to habit. He'd once had an enormous Buddha belly he often contemplated. "The only, and I mean *only* thing known that can cause a human to be completely immune to a god's energy is black jade."

*Black jade?* But he hadn't been wearing any.

*Wait.*

*Oh no.*

Her goddess blood pressure dropped to her perfect ankles. "That's it." Why hadn't she thought of it before? They'd kissed, touched, and fondled for extended periods of time, all without the aid of black jade. Mortals could not tolerate extended contact without the material. Which meant she'd neglected one important fact: Távas's body was riddled with black jade. As the Maaskab king, he would've regularly ingested the stuff to help him amp up his powers. After thousands of years, it wouldn't surprise her if the black jade had permanently settled in his bones and flesh.

"He's immune to me because he's filled with black jade."

"Whyyy…?" he asked suspiciously.

"Because…he's the Maaskab king?" She winced and then cringed on the inside as she spilled the beans. "But if I could make him forget his past, his soul would reach for the light. I know it would."

"You are mated to the most evil being on the planet?"

She nodded, crinkling her nose as if smelling something putrid.

"Wow." He raised his caramel-colored brows. "Didn't see that one coming. Is the Universe PMSing or something? Or perhaps she has had too much to drink. I, too, have done many, many stupid things when drunk—like the time I glued my naked body to the Empire State Building in the middle of January."

She remembered that. She'd had to wipe the memory of the entire island of Manhattan. Not an easy task, but far easier than unsticking Acan and his hairy nut sack from the frozen window. *The things we do for family.*

"The Universe doesn't menstruate nor partake in spirits, brother," Forgetty said, "as I'm sure you know. But, yes, I cannot for the life of me understand why she would think to pair me with such a man." Though, they did have sexual chemistry. "All the more reason for me to set out to find my own mate, unless…well…there is one way to save him."

Acan gave her a doubtful look. "Sister, I know what you're thinking, and it will never work. Our brethren will never allow him to cross over into our realm to be filled with our light."

"Why not?"

"He's the Maaskab king."

"So?" She crossed her arms.

"Uh, because he wears human teeth and thumbs as jewelry?"

True. All the Maaskab did. "Cimil does, too."

"Yes, but that's only on Halloween to ward off the evil Maaskab spirits. And let us not forget how horrible the Maaskab smell."

That was because they smeared their bodies with the blood of their victims and never bathed—something to do with boosting their powers.

"We all have our shortcomings," she argued. "You once didn't bathe for an entire century. And you wore the same pair of tighty whities for a year until you blew yourself up and had to get a new body. Then it took another decade to get you into new underwear, so yeah. I can see how you're perfect," she said sarcastically.

Acan crossed his arms over his chest. "Point taken; however, Ta'as is the most ruthless, bloodthirsty human ever to roam the earth."

"Ta'as?"

He shrugged. "That's what Cimil calls him, along with a-hole, ass banana, evil motherfucker, sadistic knob. But don't let that discourage you from falling madly in love with the one person on this planet capable of ending your existence."

"All the more reason to take the risk and convert him to our team." She took her brother's hand. "I felt his soul, Acan. I felt it searching for the light—my light. He can be saved, and that means there could be one less evil soul on the planet."

Acan took his hand back and ran it through his long brown hair. "Let us say you are right, our brethren would still never, ever, ever, ever, ever—"

"Get to the point," she spat.

"They would never grant the Maaskab king immortality. Given his powers and knowledge, imagine what he could do if we filled him full of our light."

Their light did add to a person's strength, so Acan had a point, but... "I know, in my heart of hearts, in my soul of souls, in my flower of flowers—"

"Yes, yes. I get the point."

"I know Távas has good inside him," she argued. "And I know he's been waiting for over two thousand years to be freed from his curse."

Acan looked down at his bare feet.

*Wow. Bare everything.* "Hey, you forgot your pants again. And your underpants."

"It's Wednesday. I tend to fall back into old habits in the middle of the week. Plus, Cimil encourages us all to be evil on this day." Acan shrugged. "As for the king, I'm sorry, sister. As much as I love you, you're fighting a battle that cannot be won."

She grabbed his arm so hard that it triggered a yelp. "You of all people should know that there's no such thing. Otherwise, why call it a battle? Why not a picnic? Or a hug fest? Battles are meant to be fought until one side loses, and we both know that fate decides the winner."

"That skanky, lying whore?" Acan scoffed.

"No. I don't mean our sister. I mean the real fate, the cosmic flow of energy that directs us all toward our higher purpose."

"I like that one. It's amazing how it tells you how much mustard to put on a sandwich."

She shook her head. "Whatever you say. But I need your help to convince our brethren to accept Távas into our realm to heal him."

"What if Távas is tricking you? Because, allow me to remind you, we've fallen for his traps in the past."

He had another point. "Then I guess we have to ask ourselves which is the higher risk? Falling for his trap or failing to cure him. Because sooner or later, he will rebuild his army. He will best us again." Távas had done it once before, trapping nearly all of the gods in a cenote—a freshwater pool they used as a portal to their world—for over seventy years. In the gods' absence, the Maaskab grew more powerful. "I vote we cure him."

Acan scratched his balls.

"Stop that!" She slapped his arm. "It's so disgusting."

"Sorry. Balls itch. Especially when one is thinking about such complex issues."

"You're such a weirdo." It was then that Forgetty realized that Louie had been standing there the entire time with his mouth open and his dark eyes nearly popping from his head.

"Don't worry," she said to Louie, "I'll make sure you forget this. Especially the ball itching." Otherwise, the poor kid would have nightmares for the rest of his life.

"As for you," she pointed to Acan, "send out the flare—emergency meeting over at the Immortal Matchmakers office. Tonight."

"Cimil has already called a meeting."

*Good, she'll be there. Because I have a fucking score to settle with that bitch.*

"What did she call the meeting for?" Forgetty asked.

"Your guess is as good as mine."

# CHAPTER FIFTEEN

Forgetty did not know what to expect when she got
into the elevator, heading for the fourteenth floor of
the downtown LA office building, the official home
of Immortal Matchmakers, Inc., run by Cimil and
Zac, which was sometimes used for emergency
meetings such as this. However, the last time she'd
been to this office for a summit, she'd ended up
decapitated by Acan. He'd been in the process of
flipping and had lost control, which became the
turning point in his journey toward accepting
Margarita, his lovely new wife.

*Well, let's hope this meeting goes a bit smoother.*
Though, she knew for certain at least one head was
going to roll.

Forgetty poked the button. "Can't this thing go
any faster?"

After a minute, the elevator slowed and the
doors slid open. She stepped out into the giant
office that had far too little furniture—a few desks,
filing cabinets, and a lunch table and sofa—given
the football-field-size space.

Cimil, Roberto, and some of her other brethren
and their mates stood around a big foldout table in

the center of the gray carpeted room, sipping cocktails.

Her hate-filled eyes zeroed right onto Cimil. *Lying, manipulative, heartless dick!* Forgetty couldn't wait for the meeting to start and for everyone to hear her story. *Cimil's reign of terror ends tonight!*

Forgetty felt instantly relieved to see a few allies in the room. Acan and Margarita—a fit blonde beauty in her mid-forties—served Acan's famous flaming mojitos from a makeshift bar created from a bookshelf. Also in the room were Antonio, a lovely Spanish incubus, and Ixy, the Goddess of Happiness—*so nice to see her in a sundress.* Literally, it had little yellow suns all over it. Ixy used to be the Goddess of Suicide, only wearing black lace over her face, until she discovered she had the ability to gobble up bad energy and turn it into happiness.

And, of course, there was the human-born Goddess of Love, Ashli—a lovely part Asian, part Haitian woman—who'd married Forgetty's brother Máax, the God of Time Travel. He used to be invisible, but now he was a devoted father who left the godly duties to Ashli since he was only permitted to use his powers for emergencies. *Time Travel and Love. Mated. Who wudda thunk it?*

As for the rest of the gods in attendance, all one had to do was imagine a room full of the tallest, best-looking people in the universe, and that was a summit.

All right. And add a handful of tablets around

the table, a fairly recent addition to their meetings for those who couldn't come in person. Votan, the God of Death and War, with his long, flowing blue-black hair, and his beautiful red-haired wife Emma, for example, lived in New York with their children. Their tablet only displayed a blank wall, which meant they were likely making out while waiting for the meeting to commence.

Also joining remotely was the dark-haired part-angel Penelope, who now served as the Ruler of the House of Gods—basically she ran their meetings and took notes. Her hubby, the ex-Sun God, was probably lurking somewhere in the background.

Forgetty guessed the conference-call speaker in the center of the table was for everyone else not present visually, like Akna, the Goddess of Fertility, or Bees, the Mistress of…yep! Bees!

*Speaking of bees…* The room was abuzz with the latest gossip, everyone speculating as to why Cimil had called the meeting.

Forgetty, in a pair of old jeans, a plain white T-shirt, and flip-flops—today called for casual comfort—marched over to the bar. "Hey, Acan. Hi, Margarita. Can I have a tall glass of vodka with one ice cube and a twist of lime?"

The two looked at her.

"What?" she asked.

Acan, who wore his light brown hair in a man bun tonight, shrugged his bare shoulders.

Forgetty could only surmise he was nude on the

other side of the makeshift bar. Lucky him to have found a mate who rolled with his eccentricities.

"It's just…you never drink that," he said. "And tonight, it's not your perfect drink."

*Ah, yes.* As God of Wine, he could look at anyone and know what beverage perfectly complemented their life in that exact moment.

"Yeah, well," she said, "it's what I drink at every summit. You just don't remember."

He frowned with those turquoise eyes—same as hers and all the other gods'. "Not true. I remember every drink you've had since birth—wine, wine, wine, wine, wine—okay, a few thousand years of wine since that's all there was—followed by a lot of beer, then pulque, tequila, hard cider, the first form of vodka, fermented mangos, figs, pears, and jellybean liqueur. Oh, let us not forget the birth of the grain alcohols, in which case your favorites were whiskey, grog, and—"

"Okay." Forgetty held out her palm. "How do you know all that? Did you write it down?"

Acan looked at Margarita, a blonde with radiant skin and a killer body, wearing Spandex running pants and a tank.

The two of them shook their heads, clearly confused.

"I don't know what you mean, sister," Acan said. "Why wouldn't I remember your bar list? It is my gift, as you well know."

Forgetty stepped back, nearly tripping on the

back of her flip-flop. "I-I don't understand." *How could he possibly remember such details?*

"Hey, Forgetty. How you been since the incident?" said her sister Ixy—the one in the sundress, her long dark hair braided down her back.

"Sorry?" Forgetty said.

Ixy leaned forward. "You know," she pointed at Acan, "when Belchy-boy there lost his shit and treated us all like bowling balls at his personal alley."

Forgetty slowly shook her head from side to side. "How do you remember that—I mean, the part where I'm in it?" she whispered.

Confusion sparked in Ixy's turquoise eyes. "How could I not? Hey, are you feeling all right?"

What was happening? It was like some bizarre episode of *Black Mirror*, where some alternate reality had taken hold. *Only it's missing the psycho, knife-toting Rumba.* And in this episode, everyone suddenly remembered her with a level of detail she'd never experienced.

"Everyone," called out Cimil, clanking her cocktail glass with a pen.

*Jeez. What the hell is on the front of her shirt?* The tee had a picture of a bunch of dead dolphins or sharks or something, hanging by their tails on a dock, while she gave the hang loose sign with her hand. The caption said, "Don't mess with a mess." Roberto wore a strange white samurai robe. They were both nuts.

"It's time to get this shit-show on the road," said

Cimil, placing her hand in the crook of Roberto's arm.

Forgetty slowly raised her hand. "Shouldn't the others leave? Because only those with a vote can be present. It's the law." Forgetty didn't want Roberto stepping in when it came time to argue her case and expose Cimil. She already had an uphill battle simply to convince a majority of fourteen gods to side with her.

"She is correct," said Penelope, the Spanish-looking brunette with long silky hair, her full face displayed on the tablet. "As Ruler of the House of Gods, I must ask those in the room without a vote to leave unless they are pertinent to the topic of discussion, in which case, they may wait outside until they are summoned."

With a jerk of Cimil's head, Roberto reluctantly turned to leave.

As she slid into her foldout chair, Forgetty noted that Roberto had weapons under his robe. *Cimil's up to something. She always is.* But tonight, Forgetty would remind everyone how Cimil had betrayed them a thousand times, hurt them in unthinkable ways. *And they call Távas evil.*

The room cleared of nonessential mates, and Penelope cleared her throat. "I hereby call this emergency summit to order. Present are thirteen of the fourteen gods. Missing is Zac, God of Temptation. Meeting has been called by Cimil, the Goddess of—"

"I, too, called this meeting." Forgetty raised her hand. "Cimil just beat me to it."

Cimil didn't react.

"And your emergency?" Penelope asked.

Those seated at the table turned to look at Forgetty with curiosity.

*What in the world?* They weren't just looking at her; they saw her. Really saw her. *Fucking hell. This is strange.*

"Well, sweetie?" prodded Penelope. "What is it? You never ask for anything, so it must be important."

Unused to being treated like a real deity, Forgetty gave her head a little shake before lifting her chin. *Here we go.* "The Universe has chosen the King of the Maaskab as my mate. He's thwarted my transition to evil, which has saved billions of humans from immeasurable suffering. As a reward for his actions, I am here to petition for his immortal soul."

A unified gasp exploded from every mouth in and out of the room, followed by a loud cough from Cimil. "Hack-hack. Looney alert."

*Oh, bring it, you wacko, garage-sale mon! 'Cause it's on!* Forgetty scowled at Cimil, who sat directly across the table. "Why don't you shut your lie hole, skank."

"My, my. Such aggressiveness," Cimil mock whined. "But what can we expect from someone mated to a Maaskab, a man who has sworn to end us all?"

*There. Right there. That's the backstabbing Cimil everyone needs to see.*

"Fuck you, sister," Forgetty spat. "I've stood by you for longer than even *I* can remember. But tonight that ends. It ended the moment you told me that I was unlovable, undeserving of a mate and destined for eternity to be a spinster. What you've done was downright unforgiveable. Especially since I've been nothing but good to you."

Cimil chuckled and then made a circle around her temple. "Crazy talk. Never mind her."

"No!" Forgetty slammed her fist onto the table, nostrils flared. "I've suffered immeasurably. And just when I couldn't take any more, I bellied up to the bar and asked for another sour serving." Forgetty looked around the table at the astonished faces. "I. Have. Given. Everything. To you, to this world, and to my job. I never expected a mate or love or even the simple kindnesses bestowed upon familiar strangers, such as cool birthday cards with sparkly unicorns or pink fuzzy slippers from Santa. But to be betrayed by my own sister?" Her fists clenched. "I expected you, Cimil, at the very fucking least, to have my motherfucking back."

Cimil's jaw remained poised, as did the rest of her traitorous body. "Well, wasn't that a colorful, expletive-filled speech?" She began to clap and chuckle, looking around the room for support.

It didn't come.

Meanwhile, Forgetty's veins flowed with liquid

fire. "Your time of reckoning is here, sister. You've pulled the wool over our eyes long enough, and you've used your otherworldly charms to blind us for the last time." Forgetty stood, digging her fingernails into the plastic table. "As for why you've brought us here and your supposed emergency, I couldn't give a million expletives about a single syllable, let alone an entire word, coming from your lying mouth. I vote to remove Cimil from the agenda along with her from our lives."

Cimil rose in indignation. "I have done nothing but serve and ensure this world continues."

Coughs of protest erupted around the table.

"There. You see?" said Forgetty. "They know. And so do I."

"You're creating a drama mountain out of a drama molehill," Cimil said. "And boohoo. So I didn't tell you that Ta'as is your mate."

"Távas," Forgetty corrected.

Cimil flared her nostrils. "I like to say it with a twang, and the last time I checked, twanging was still a god's given right—at least in Texas, which is the singular authority on twanging and other sexy cowboy-esque drawls."

Forgetty rolled her eyes. "Moron." *Though, Texas clearly does have a leg up in the drawl department.*

"No. *You* are the moron," Cimil charged at her verbally. "Because I called this meeting to let everyone know that the Maaskab king—your sweetie pie—plus his few remaining minions, have already recruited two hundred new members. And by recruited, I mean he kidnapped them, injected them with black jade, and then gave them the evil whammy. By tomorrow, their numbers will be up to a thousand. Next month, ten thousand. War is imminent unless I'm given back my powers so I can stop it."

Everyone stared at Cimil in silence, and if Forgetty had to guess, she would say they were all thinking the exact same thing.

"I'm calling bullshit." Forgetty crossed her arms over her chest.

Cimil flashed a coy smile. "I thought you all might need proof." She turned her head. "Roberto! Bring in the Scab!"

"Scab" was short for Maaskab, which was why the gods in attendance had a huge unanimous hissy, ranging from gasps to "are you out of your mind?"

Roberto sifted into the room, depositing a massive, nearly seven-foot-tall Maaskab decked out in full evil-Mayan-priest regalia, which included a loincloth made of human skin, soot and blood-caked skin, and the trademark thumb necklace. His hair, however, was unusually short for a Scab, so while it looked nappy, it lacked the standard dreads beaded with human teeth.

*Wait. Is that…Távas?*

"Someone get the air freshener!" called out Ashli, the coco-skinned Goddess of Love. "He smells like death warmed over in a crockpot."

The Scab's eyes, which were pits of blood red and black, went straight to Forgetty.

*Oh, Jesus.* In the past, when she'd come across these horrifying monsters, her instincts had told her to strike hard and then run. But that fear didn't come, like she expected. All she could think of was reaching for him. It filled her heart with heavy dread to see him forced to be something she now believed he was not.

"What did she do to you, Távas?" Forgetty whispered.

"I didn't do squat!" Cimil said. "He's evil. He's been recruiting, and he's come to confess."

*Confess?* Maaskab didn't confess. They fought to the death. It was totally their thing.

Távas cleared his throat. "It is true." His voice came out like rusty razor blades scraping across a sheet of steel, making everyone shriek. His mouth oozed with dark gooey slime—the result of having ingested copious amounts of black jade, no doubt. "I have been building an army. So while you may have gotten lucky and captured me, my men have been well trained. They know how to evade you, and by week's end, we will be a thousand strong."

*I smell a rat! Okay, and ripe death mixed with stale BO.* Damn, Távas really needed a shower. But that didn't matter now. What did was that her connection to this monster felt blocked, or, or…she didn't really know. *Something is off.* Yes, there was darkness inside him, but underneath all the layers was a light he didn't want her to see. She literally felt him pushing her away with everything he had.

*It's his heart.* It was beating with love. *So much love.*

Forgetty stood and pointed across the table at Cimil. "You've staged this. You're forcing him to say these things. I can feel it." She looked at the monster before her. "What did Cimil threaten you with, Távas? Or did she promise you something, like she'd look after Louie if she got her powers back? Or maybe—wait." Távas's words fully sank in. Forgetty looked back at Cimil. "Where's this army? Huh?"

"I dunno." Cimil shrugged. "But if I'm given back my powers, I will—"

"There is no army," Forgetty snarled. "Nor can there be until the plague has passed."

"What do you mean, sister?" said Ashli.

"Well, unless Távas was able to find individuals who are mated, and therefore immune to the plague, anyone given the evil whammy at this point in time will actually just turn out super nice. Like Cimil's nanny."

Cimil's jaw dropped. "Well, well, yes. That is exactly what Távas did. He found married men and then gave them a scabby makeover. Right, king of the Maaskab?"

Távas stood there, trading glances between Forgetty and Cimil.

*Man, his eyes are creepy.* Forgetty wished someone had brought sunglasses for him.

"Well, I, uh…" Távas's scary raspy voice tapered off.

"Tell them the truth, Távas," Forgetty urged, pulling on the threads that bound them. "Because whatever Cimil has promised you, she will betray you. She can't be trusted. But I can. You know I can."

He sighed with exasperation, making his soot-covered shoulders rise slowly, followed by a heavy drop.

Just then, the elevator doors slid open and out walked Zac carrying a petite limp body in his arms.

"Cimil!" he roared, storming toward the table, shirtless, barefoot, and wearing only his standard-issue black leather pants. "You fucking bitch. I'm going to kill you." He laid the body down at the head of the table just as Cimil jumped up and Roberto protectively sifted in front of her.

*Oh no. Tula.* Forgetty cupped her hands over her mouth. The body was lifeless, her sweet, sweet face blue.

"What happened?" Forgetty asked, while the other gods gasped in horror.

"Good freaking question. What did you do to her?" Cimil asked Zac.

Like a bolt of lightning, Zac moved around Roberto and grabbed Cimil by the throat.

"Back off!" Roberto, who was far faster, pulled Zac away and sent him flying across the open room.

Zac landed on his back with a thud but was on his feet in a split second, rushing at Cimil again like a rabid dog.

"Wait!" Forgetty ran to block him. "Tell us what happened, Zac. Because if you harm Cimil, you'll be dragged away and no one will know. She'll just continue doing what she's always done—hurt us."

With fists clenched and his face filled with the sort of rage fueled by a soul on fire, Zac's chest heaved. "She killed Tula."

"I did not!" Cimil protested.

Zac pointed at Cimil over Forgetty's shoulder. "You lied. You told me that Tula would die if I ever allowed myself to love her."

"Well, obviously I was right!" Cimil replied, bouncing on her toes, trying to see over Roberto's huge body.

"No. You deceived me! You made me believe that my love would poison her, so I closed my heart to her love." Zac went on to tell everyone what had happened, including killing mermen and how it had all led to Tula's death. "Had you not lied to me, sister," he said, his turquoise eyes red with tears, "had I just accepted Tula, I never would have flipped. And she would still be alive."

Cimil huffed. "You can't blame me for your choices! You know I'm a liar. It's how I roll!"

Suddenly, the table split in two and crashed to the floor. Tula's body was gone.

The gods on the speakerphone and tablets all freaked out, yelling and trying to ascertain what had happened. Their communication devices were scattered across the floor.

"Minky! Is that you?" said Cimil. "Spit Tula's body out this instant. It's rude to eat people's dead mates. And where were you? Roberto and I came to free you from those horrible mermen, but you were already gone."

Cimil listened to what sounded like complete silence to the rest of them.

"No, Minky," said Cimil. "Not you, too. I didn't betray you."

Silence.

"You wanted to hide from me on that island? But why, Minky?" Cimil's eyes teared.

The elevator doors slid open and out stepped…

*Uh-oh. Mermen,* Forgetty thought.

"This summit meeting just got way more awesome," said Ashli, the Goddess of Love, to her sister Ixy, the Goddess of Happiness.

"Seriously. Best meeting ever." Ixy grinned.

Roen, king of the mermen, had on a sleek black suit, the expensive kind he wore when appearing on those fancy rich-guy magazines. He had been the quintessential playboy billionaire for years before he learned of his supernatural bloodline. Now he was living a dual life, like Batman.

*Only mermen are way bigger badasses,* Forgetty thought as ten large men, also dressed in expensive threads, emerged from the elevator, flanking Roen.

"How did they all fit inside there?" asked Acan to no one in particular.

"When you look that hot," said Ashli, "you can fit into all the tight spaces you like."

"Hey. I'm right here. Your hot husband, remember?" said Máax, your typical attractive deity with golden brown hair, olive skin, and the god eyes.

She shrugged. "Sorry. Can't help it. I'm the Goddess of Love. Lust is a precursor."

"Will someone please lock that elevator before the Loch Ness Monster or Cookie Monster shows up next?" Cimil said. "Our meeting has clearly reached maximum monster capacity."

"You!" Roen pointed at Cimil. "You will pay for what you have done!"

"*Moi?*" Cimil innocently pointed at herself from behind the safety of Roberto's hulking body.

Roen's green eyes flickered with rage. "Minky told us what you did to your brother Zac, and we know it was you who came to our island today and killed three of my men."

"I did no such thing!" Cimil stepped out from behind Roberto. "Why is everyone trying to frame me? I will not stand for it."

"What's that on your shirt?" Acan asked.

Cimil's usually pale face turned a startling shade of shame red as her eyes slowly glided down to the picture on her chest of her posing in front of three finned creatures suspended by their tails in the background.

*Oh. I guess those weren't dolphins.*

"You…made…a shirt?" Roen thundered.

"Well, I-I-I, uh…" Cimil stuttered.

"It's over, Cimil. Over." Roen and his men encircled Roberto and Cimil. "And you should know I have an army at your house. If you run, you'll never see your children again."

"You have my kids?" Cimil shrieked.

"They are extremely frightening, so we do not wish to keep them, but yes, they are in our custody. And Minky has agreed to take them away if you do not do as we ask."

"Whoa. Whoa. You can't take my kids." Cimil looked around the faces in the room, but found no sympathy. "I have an explanation for everything I've done, and besides, whatever happened to due-god-process, huh? Also, you can't afford to lose me. A war is coming. A big ugly war. Without me and my powers, you're all toast!"

"There is no threat from us." Távas spoke up, running his large hands through his sticky short hair with an uncomfortable wince. Real Maaskab didn't feel discomfort, only hunger. "It is as Aurora said, we cannot create an army at this time. Anyone Cimil forced me to convert just wants to knit scarves for wayward kittens and volunteer for charities."

"Who is Aurora?" asked Acan.

"Me. It's my name." Forgetty spoke up.

"It's quite lovely," said Roen.

"Thank you," she replied and then turned to the horrific monster who owned her heart.

He stared with sincerity from behind his bloody eyes. "I am sorry, Aurora. Cimil promised if I helped her get her powers back, she would make me a demigod so I would change."

"To good?" Forgetty placed her hand over her heart.

He nodded. "Do not get me wrong; I really enjoy spreading darkness and despair around the world. I'm very good at it. And nobody can rip out a heart like me. But," he drew a breath, "I would give it all up just to be with you, to see you happy. And to be a good father to Louie."

"Who's Louie?" whispered Ashli.

"His son. He lives with me now," Aurora replied.

"It's just another lie," argued Cimil. "And who are you going to believe, a Scab or me?"

"Scab," everyone replied in unison.

"Hey! Will someone please put my tablet back on the table?" Penelope yelled. "I can't see shit, and this all sounds like a delicious soap opera that comes along only once in a lifetime."

Máax grabbed her tablet and held it up. "Sorry. Table is totaled." He turned the tablet to face out so the room could see Penelope.

"Thank you, Máax," Penelope said. "So, in light

of this new information, I move that Cimil be taken into custody and put on trial. Again."

Everyone groaned. They'd all been to this rodeo.

"No." Roen stepped forward. "She committed a crime on our soil, on our island, where I rule. She murdered my men in cold blood. These were good men with mates and children."

Cimil pointed at Zac. "He killed five of them."

Zac snarled. "Backstabbing, traitorous—"

"But it was you, Cimil, who initiated the chain of events." Roen shook his head. "Zac was merely your puppet."

"Oh, whatever. So I killed a few fishies. The gods don't care," Cimil spouted.

"Yes, they do." Aurora stepped forward. "What are you proposing?" she asked Roen.

"For her crimes, she is to be placed inside a steel drum that will be filled with cement and dropped to the bottom of the ocean in an undisclosed location."

"Nobody is touching my pregnant wife," Roberto snarled, reaching for something beneath his robe. "Not unless you want a war with the vampires, who, might I remind you, serve as the strongest part of your army."

"Pregnant?" a small voice came out of the speaker on the floor. "She can't be pregnant."

Aurora reached for the device and held it u- "What did you say, Akna?" Akna was the God of Fertility. She was likely off in some cave she wouldn't cause major damage. Two seconds in a room with her was said to inflict quadruplets, even in the elderly and inanimate objects. *It's like she's the opposite of me.* Everyone remembered Akna—then tried to stay the hell away.

"Cimil can't be pregnant," Akna said. "I mean, at least I don't think so. She couldn't get pregnant on her own last time, so I had to help her. And I haven't seen Cimil for months."

"I've been taking my vitamins!" Cimil argued.

"Is this true, Cimil?" Roberto's nostrils flared. "You lied to me about being pregnant?"

"No. I didn't. I really am," Cimil argued.

"You wanted me to help you get your powers back." Roberto stepped back from Cimil. "That's what this was all about."

"No. No, honey. I would never lie to you." She paused. "Okay. That's another lie because we both know I totally would, but I'm not lying about this." She threw up her arms. "I mean, what reason would I have to deceive you? You knew I wanted my powers back."

"Yes, and I agreed; however, that was to save our unborn children—who, by the way, do not exist. Otherwise, I wouldn't have agreed. I know you make everything worse when you meddle. But now I see, Cimil, it was all a ruse." Roberto looked at Roen. "Take her."

"Roberto?" Cimil's face contorted with shock.

Roberto held out his large hand. "Lying to a

man about his babies is crossing the line. From this day forward, you are dead to me, Cimil. I disavow you as my mate, as the mother of my children, and as my tango partner."

Cimil stood speechless, as did the rest of the room.

"Take her," Roen said to his men.

"Wait," said Aurora. "I think we're all forgetting something. If those two aren't mated, won't they flip?"

Grumbles and side conversations erupted.

"Lock me away if you must," said Roberto. "The children and I will be better off in one of your prisons than with my *ex*-mate."

Cimil looked positively devastated, her mouth flapping. "But…I'm not lying. I am pregnant. Why won't anyone believe me?"

"Not even your vicious, sneaky, bloodthirsty, disco-loving, invisible unicorn believes you, Cimil." Roberto gave the nod, and Roen's men dragged Cimil into the stairwell.

The room fell into a cold, bitter silence, resembling a funeral. Even Aurora felt the pangs of mourning. Had they made the right decision?

Somehow, it didn't feel like it.

# CHAPTER SIXTEEN

After Cimil's departure, everyone helped to get the room back together. The LA platoon of the gods' mortal army, known as Uchben, had been called in to take Távas. To everyone's surprise, he did not resist. And Roberto, who was far too powerful to let flip and roam free, would go with them. Both men would be transported to Sedona, Arizona, where the Uchben had an underground prison for immortals. There was also a lovely spa, gym, underground shopping mall, and bocce ball. Okay, really it was like a resort, but with maximum security. Acan, before finding his mate, had spent a considerable amount of time there for repeated violations of just about every law imaginable, so he'd made it a point to liven up the place, being the party god and all.

"Be sure to feed my children before you attempt to transport them," Roberto said as he got into the elevator with the soldiers and Távas. "Otherwise, they might chew a few heads."

"Head chewing." Távas chuckled, standing next to Roberto. "Haven't seen that one for a while. Is it a thing again?"

"Ha!" Who knew Maaskab could make jokes?

Aurora laughed and then flashed a smile at Távas. She wanted him to see that she felt confident in what came next: Convincing the gods to let him become a demigod. After all, he'd come clean and confessed to Cimil's plot. He'd shown them all that he was capable of doing right.

Now the only question was if they believed his past could be just that. His past. Obviously, she had a direct line to his soul. She knew the truth of him. The danger was that they might see her connection as one that blinded her judgment versus illuminated reality.

"Wait!" She stood from her chair and bolted to the elevator, shoving her hand between the doors.

"Goddess, what are you doing?" snarled one of the soldiers dressed in black cargos and a black tee—the standard Uchben uniform.

"Just give me five minutes." She held up her fingers to the soldiers. "Five. I'm going to question him." If she used their bond to push the right buttons, she'd get to the bottom of Távas's story and, therefore, his true nature.

"Aurora, don't. You'll only end up disappointed," Távas said.

She pointed at Távas's face. "There, you see, everyone. The fact that he cares about my well-being is proof: He's not all bad."

Hesitant looks exchanged between the faces in the room.

"Fine. Okay." She threw up her hands. "I know

that Távas, aka Ta'as, aka Satan's tutor, Mr. Motherfucking Bastard, King Scab, Jerktoes—"

"Woman…" growled Távas, now standing off to the side of the room with the soldiers next to him, "get on with it."

"Yes, yes. Okay." She drew a fortifying breath and went to stand at the head of the table to more easily see everyone. She raised her arm and pointed at Távas. "The truth is, this man has tormented us for over two millennia. He has murdered countless humans. He is the embodiment of evil—"

"Have you ever considered law school?" asked Ashli, the Goddess of Love, seated directly next to her.

"No," replied Aurora. "Why?"

"Just making sure. Please keep it that way."

Aurora gave her a sharp look. "Okay, I know what you're all thinking, but consider the bigger picture. If we can take someone as powerful as Távas and get him to play for Team Good, think about the implications. He's a wealth of knowledge, the first astrophysicist ever. He's the first quantum physicist, too. He invented the means for time travel, he discovered black jade, and he can possess thousands of people. The wealth of knowledge inside this man could be the only defense we have against an age of humans we do not understand. I mean…come on? Memes. What's that all about? Snapchat. So you want to see your friends with goofy noses? We used to call that Halloween.

Instagram? Pictures of your life—a thing no one used to need because humans actually hung out together." Forgetty pointed to the faces around the room. "We are no longer equipped to serve humanity because the internet has allowed humans to praise, spit, judge, love, like, and kick with the stroke of a finger. Távas is a strategic genius. His devious mind could help us think of devious ways to help keep humanity on track."

Aurora looked around the room, spotting one hand raised. Her brother with the giant man bun.

"Acan, what's your question?" she asked.

"I just want to know one thing. How did he become evil? And why, if he truly has a good heart, he stayed that way? All right, those are two questions. But so be it. I'm a rebel and have accepted my lot."

Aurora puckered her lips and placed one hand on her hip before turning her gaze to the giant sooty monster watching her with hungry eyes.

Her stomach flipped. Even in his roadkill ensemble, he actually sort of did it for her. "Well, Távas? It's now or never. Time to come clean."

Távas stared for a long moment, his blood-red eyes swirling with black like an ominous lava lamp.

Finally, he stepped forward, eliciting multiple yelps.

"Well," he said, his deep, deep voice sounding like James Earl Jones with a throat cold, "I was born a slave. No, not even that. I was the son of a slave of a slave, as was customary in the Mayan culture. A servant of a prominent family could buy his own servants to help with the farm and household chores. My mother and father served the master slave. And when I was old enough, I served him, too."

Forgetty knew this was true. Though the Mayans were a culture close to the gods' hearts, because of their thirst for science and knowledge in general, they were also a violent people who had no qualms about oppressing others. The Maaskab were the offspring of this barbaric, bloodthirsty culture.

Távas went on. "It was when I turned sixteen that a plague of locusts wiped out our crops and the priests in the village demanded sacrifices to appease the gods." His eyes flickered to solid coal-mine black. "They wanted young males, who they believed would feed the God of Corn and produce hearty crops."

"Which one of us is the God of Corn?" asked Acan. "I hope it's not me."

"No. Shush!" Aurora said. The Mayans were notorious for making shit up. "What did you do?" she asked Távas, urging him to continue.

"I went with the priests, but they did not kill me. Their leader saw potential, likely because of my unusually large size and strength. He said I glowed with life. So he began to train me—making me sacrifice animals and eat their organs for sustenance, then forcing me to fast for weeks and locking me in their dark prayer room."

"Why would he do that?" Aurora asked.

"He believed that when one was on death's doorstep, deprived of anything connected to this world, they could speak to the gods."

"Obviously bullshit," she said.

"Yes, but when I was finally let out, delirious with hunger, he beat me until I said what he wanted to hear: That the gods told me more sacrifices were required to save our people from starvation. So I said it. And then I regretted it. Because they didn't come for me, as I'd hoped. They came for my family, including my baby brother."

The room filled with tension, everyone sitting at the edges of their seats.

He went on, "When it came time for my mother's heart to be torn out over the altar at Chichen Itza—"

"You ate it?" piped Ixy.

"No." Távas frowned. "What sort of monster do you think I am? I lunged for the head priest and pushed him down the stairs. Then I claimed the gods had granted me the power to kill him. They all believed me, and the rest is history."

"So…" Penelope spoke up over her tablet. "From there, you just…got all wicked and bloodthirsty for no reason?"

"I was young. The other priests resented me, and for survival, and the survival of my family, I had to maintain power. I had to become the monster I am today. But that required effort and sacrifices. Yes, the bloody kind. When I eventually discovered black jade, completely by accident, I saw it as a means to demonstrate my authority. One of the priests had ingested it, believing it was charcoal—a common remedy in those days for an upset stomach. I noticed he was unusually susceptible to my commands, so I made a few more priests ingest black jade. From there, it spiraled. People saw my power and demanded I give them prosperity. 'Make it rain, bring the crops, sacrifice more slaves,' they demanded. We even went to war with other tribes to take what we did not have. My army and people became more and more bloodthirsty and power hungry, as did I. That was when I began my research on dark energy and discovered how to harness it. But this thirst would be our downfall. The people began turning on each other. Those who could escape did. The families who remained killed each other off. One day, I woke and there was nothing left but me." He looked down at his large hands. "The unspeakable things I did to save my family were necessary. But once they were gone, I had only myself to blame. Like my people, I too became addicted to power."

Aurora sank into her chair at the head of the table. That had been one hell of a story, but something didn't make sense. He'd started on his journey for his family; however, once they were saved, he could've taken them and run instead of continuing with the charade. He hadn't become evil or addicted to power yet, so he must've had some reason to stay.

"Why didn't you walk away?" Aurora asked. "Initially, I mean. Right after you saved your family?"

"I couldn't," he replied.

"But why?" she demanded, sensing the tender light in his heart fighting to expose itself.

"I cannot say."

He could say. He simply didn't want to.

She drew a slow breath and exhaled. "Then you will die, Távas. And my heart along with you."

He looked away, and she could see the turmoil stirring inside him, swirls of white mixing with dark blues.

*What's he hiding?*

"Távas, you've been a powerful king for thousands of years. Yet you don't have the courage to face your demons?"

He didn't respond.

"Távas? I'm begging. Down on my knees if I must."

His gaze whipped in her direction. "To save your precious humans, no doubt."

"No." She spoke softly. "To save you."

His eyes flickered to a crisp blue.

"Tell us why," she pleaded, "you didn't run after your family was safe?"

He swallowed, the room cocooned in absolute stillness. "Because the rave tour wasn't the first time we've met, Aurora."

"It wasn't?" she asked.

"No. I met you over two thousand years ago, before I became what I am. I saw you come through the cenote, and it was like…" He released a slow breath. "Magic."

"That's called a boner, dude," said Acan.

"Shush!" Ashli, the Goddess of Love, barked.

Távas continued. "Coming face-to-face with a god was nothing shy of awe inspiring. But the way you looked at me, Aurora, like I wasn't there, it had quite an impact on me."

Aurora inhaled sharply. *That's where I've seen his tattoos before.* She thought she'd seen the geometric shapes on a building or painting. But she'd seen them on a young man thousands of years ago.

*Now I remember.* "I was coming through the cenote, and there was this split second, right as my body was completed, that I glanced toward the edge of the pool and saw a tall young man with the bluest eyes. When I climbed out of the water, he was gone, and I saw no evidence that he'd ever been there. Not a fleck of mud out of place." She'd never given it another thought. "I was sure you'd been a dream," she said.

"No," he said. "But you have always been mine."

The ladies in the room swooned, as did Aurora.

"So I'm the reason you stayed with your people?" If yes, she just wouldn't know what to think of it. *How horribly ironic, I suppose.* Because it would mean that she'd created him, in a backwards kind of way.

Távas nodded. "I knew a simple, uneducated slave could never have a woman like you—a goddess—so, yes, it is true: I wanted the power so I could be your equal. So that someday we might meet again and you would see me."

Obviously, his thirst for power had gone a little sideways on him. Still, it all meant that none of this was an accident.

"So you see, goddess," Távas added, "it is as I've told you. I am a bad, bad man. A greedy man. I always have been. I always will be."

"Eh-hem?" Penelope spoke.

Aurora and Távas looked at Penelope's tablet.

"As Ruler of the House of Gods, I call for a vote. Do we grant Távas immortality? Or do we make him live out his life in a jail cell? Those who vote immortality, please raise their hands."

Aurora, Acan, and Ashli, the Goddess of Love, raised their hands.

*Only three?* Aurora's heart sank. Her plan had failed. The gods didn't see him as a person worthy of redemption and healing. They only saw a monster.

*The human-skin thong he's wearing probably isn't helping.*

"Three yeses," said Penelope. "Going once. Going twice—"

"Come on, people," Aurora pleaded, "he's no worse than Cimil. Or Roberto or...really, any of us. We've all done bad things. We all have our dark sides—I mean, Acan there literally ripped all our heads off in the last meeting. We've all killed for the people we've loved, though, granted that is our role as gods. But who's to say that he wasn't a necessary evil? Without him, black jade wouldn't have been discovered and many of you would still be single. Right?"

No reply.

"Fine," Aurora continued, refusing to accept defeat. "Máax, God of Time Travel, you wouldn't even have a title if it weren't for Távas. He figured out how to harness enough energy to propel someone through the fabric of time, which means Ashli would be dead. Like, dead dead." She'd died accidentally multiple times while Máax was attempting to court her—a long, clumsy love story. Luckily, Máax had been able to unwind the clock and have several do-overs until he got it right. All very romantic when one thought about it.

Máax and Ashli exchanged loving glances, and Aurora felt the room warming up.

"Come on, guys," she pleaded. "Even you, Votan, have to admit that you wouldn't be with Emma if the Maaskab hadn't trapped you in a cenote using black jade jars." Emma, for very complicated reasons, had been the only one able to hear Votan during his entrapment, which nearly drove her mad, but ultimately got them together. She went to free Votan and the rest was history.

Votan's screen remained blank, but lip-smacking sounds could be heard coming from his tablet.

"We'll take that as a yes," Aurora said. "All I'm asking for is that Távas and I have the same chance you've been given, as improbable of a couple as we are."

"Final vote," Penelope called out.

Four more hands rose.

*Seven.*

"Fuck." Aurora dropped her head. She needed eight. This couldn't be happening.

"It is all right, Aurora," Távas said, his deep voice filled with regret. "I do not deserve you. I do not even deserve the dream of you. Not after the things I've done. But I will spend eternity dreaming of what might have been."

"Excuse me." Ixy, the Goddess of Happiness, raised her hand. "But maybe I'm confused. You're asking for Távas to become a demigod, right?"

Aurora nodded.

"But he's filled with enough black jade and evil to light up hell for the next eternity. No—not a question. That was a statement."

Aurora nodded again.

"Okay, so why would we vote yes?" Ixy asked. "That would be negligent."

"Thanks, Ixy. Remind me to erase my memory

of you after this meeting," Aurora muttered.

"Don't get your goddess panties all ruffled, Getty," Ixy argued. "The issue is he's bad to the bone, and taking him to our realm to be filled with divine light can't possibly cure someone as evil and wicked as him."

"Your point?" Aurora asked.

"I can't give him our light, but I can try to cure him," Ixy offered.

*Jesus. Why didn't I think of that?*

Aurora's eyes filled with tears and her lower lip quivered. "You-you'd do that for me?"

"Yes," Ixy said, "you're my sister. We don't have any idea who you are, frankly, since I am only just beginning to remember you, but I know I love you, and making you happy would only bring me joy."

"You remember me?" Aurora asked.

Unanimous nods erupted in a circle around the room.

"But how?"

"Perhaps because you're now bonded with Távas," Acan offered. He knew all about how mates affected each other. They balanced each other out. Sometimes they completely swapped powers.

Aurora finally saw it. She gave Távas her selfless goodness, and in exchange he gave her visibility. *We've brought each other into the light.*

Aurora smiled. But this time, the whole room saw it. And for the first time in her existence, no one would forget.

# CHAPTER SEVENTEEN

After the tumultuous meeting, Zac and Minky had left together. It was a somber moment, one Aurora wouldn't soon forget, when Zac sobbed into Minky's invisible mane. Really, no one knew what to say, because despite their differences, Cimil and Zac had been a team. She'd hurt him worse than she'd hurt anyone, even Roberto. Zac would never recover from such a loss—his closest friend and his mate, all in one day.

"What are they going to do?" Aurora asked Ixy, now back at Aurora's sherbet-fiesta-colored penthouse.

"I don't know, but I will visit him tomorrow and see if I can't syphon off some of his pain." Ixy began shedding her jewelry, preparing for Távas's exorcism.

"Won't you be a little full?"

"Perhaps. But Antonio has lined up a bunch of incubi for me tonight, and he, too, will dine." Antonio was half incubus, half vampire and loved to snack on bad energy, whether Ixy brought it home or he found it on his own. Although her capacity was much larger and she couldn't truly die, unlike

Antonio, it was safer for her to deal with high-risk cases like Távas and then have the incubi assist her with discharging the bad energy.

"All right," said Aurora. "I hope you have an army waiting because I have a feeling that Távas is the nuclear reactor of malevolent energy."

Ixy scoffed. "This will be a piece of cake."

"Ladies, may we get on with this?" Távas called from Aurora's bedroom.

"Coming!" The two entered her room filled with Uchben soldiers. Távas lay across Aurora's bed, still in his icky Mayan priest garb.

*And I'm gonna need new sheets.*

"Someone sounds super anxious to start his new happy life," said Ixy with a giant grin, rubbing her hands with sanitizer.

"Yes," replied Távas. "Today's delivery window for chicken wings will be closing soon."

"Sorry. Chicken wings?" Aurora asked.

"It is nearly twelve thirty, and the delivery places will soon shut down."

"Not following," she said.

"I love barbeque. But the sensation of eating something bad for me is severely handicapped by being evil. One can only truly appreciate junk food when it feels sinful, which is a challenge for obvious reasons." He gave Aurora a sharp look. "Plus, I'm feeling extremely horny for you, so…there's that."

Aurora and Ixy glanced at each other and shrugged.

"Well, then," Aurora smiled and brushed her fingertips over Távas's cheek, "good thing Louie is spending the night with Acan." Margarita would hopefully keep Louie in line. She was a very responsible mother accustomed to rebellious teenagers. And Acan. Same thing. "And once you're all cured, we'll get to work on Louie."

Távas nodded. "It is my connection that has poisoned him. If I cannot be cured, there will be little hope for him."

So the father-son connection had done this to Louie? No wonder Távas felt so guilty. *Just another sign that Távas is a good man.*

"Okeydokey." Ixy clapped her hands together. "I'm ready."

Aurora reached out and gave Ixy's arm a soft squeeze. "Thank you, sister. From the bottom of my heart."

Ixy's turquoise eyes sparkled with love. "It is my pleasure to help you." Ixy turned her head and then began to chant an ancient Mayan phrase to kick off the ceremony. "*Teen uk'al k'iinam. Teen uk'al yah. Teen uk'al k'iinam. Teen uk'al yah.*" Ixy planted her hands on Távas's chest.

He immediately cried out as if she were burning him with a branding iron.

*Oh gods.* Aurora fought the urge to touch his hand, knowing that the energy flowing through them wasn't to be disturbed. Fact was, no one really understood Ixy's gift. Not even Ixy.

Távas passed out, and Ixy went into a deep trance.

"How's it going?" Aurora asked anxiously.

Ixy's skin was turning gray—not unusual, but it meant she was almost full. Suddenly, Ixy turned coal-mine black.

"Ixy!" Aurora pushed her away, and Ixy fell to the floor, convulsing.

"What happened?" Antonio rushed into the room, his green eyes filled with panic.

"I don't know. She only touched Távas for three seconds, four tops."

"Jesus. He's poisoned her." Antonio bent down and placed his lips on Ixy, trying to syphon off the dark energy. Within a few seconds, he pushed away and fell to the floor, panting. "It's too much."

"What do we do?" Aurora asked.

"Call in the others," Antonio grumbled.

"There are only three incubi in the living room. Aren't we going to need more? Want me to call someone?"

"Who?" he sputtered.

"I don't know. Don't you guys have some sort of hotline or group page on Facebook?" Aurora asked frantically.

"No. We're not a knitting circle. And most incubi don't carry phones."

"That's strange, but whatever. We still need more—"

"There are very few of us left in the world,

thanks to you gods. So we must try with the three we have."

*Dammit.* He was right. The gods had sent most of the demons back to their realm centuries ago. A few escaped their nets, but they were too few to warrant any concern. Still, that meant there was no bad-energy-munching incubi army to fall back on.

*But why wasn't Ixy enough?* Once, the Maaskab had gotten their paws on Chaam, the God of Male Virility. He was so full of poison that they'd thought he'd never be cured. But Ixy had him all spiffy and clean within minutes. Of course, she then spent weeks in a coma, but she had gotten the job done.

*Fuck. Something is not right.*

Aurora went into the living room and retrieved the incubi, who were watching a rerun of the show *Dancing with the Stars.*

*I knew that show was evil.* "Snack time, guys!"

The men, all very handsome with green, green eyes and olive skin—a camouflage of course—came quickly and got to work, trying to drain Ixy. But as much as they could digest, it wasn't enough to put a dent in her color. The worst that could happen was Ixy would die and come right back in a new body. But for Távas, this was his only hope.

*And it's useless.* Aurora's heart sank, realizing that this meant there was no cure. He was just too darn powerful, a seemingly bottomless pit of dark energy.

Aurora sank down next to the unconscious monster on the bed and took his dirty hand. "Gods,

Távas," she whispered. "What am I going to do with you?" It wasn't that she couldn't live without him, but she didn't want to. Now that she'd had a taste of love—messy, difficult, agonizing—she never wanted to forget it. She liked that it wasn't perfect or easy to come by. The bumps, bruises, pain, and scars gave love its true beauty.

She kissed the top of his rough sticky hand, numb to the stench, because if any man could love her, he deserved her unwavering loyalty. "And you have mine, my evil, rotten king."

Távas whimpered but did not open his eyes.

❧ ❦

The next morning, Aurora woke to a very dirty and very empty bed. The Uchben soldiers were sprawled out on the floor of her bedroom, unconscious.

*Oh no.* She ran over to check them out. Their auras had flecks of black, but they didn't appear to be injured, just in a very deep sleep.

*Maaskab mind control.* It would likely wear off.

"Távas?" She got to her feet and bolted to the bathroom, only to find it empty. She went into the living room, where she found Ixy, Antonio, and the three incubi all piled in a heap on the orange carpet, looking like they'd had some sort of clothed orgy before passing out.

"Ixy!" Aurora gave her sister a shake, noting her skin tone had returned to a pinkish hue.

"What?" Ixy groaned.

"What happened? Where's Távas?"

Ixy's bright blue-green eyes popped open. "What do you mean?"

"He's not here, and the soldiers have been put under—like some sort of napping spell."

Ixy sat up, rubbing the back of her head. "The next time I offer to help out a Scab, please shoot me in the face—it would feel way better."

"Do you remember anything?" Aurora asked.

"Not after I passed out."

Aurora had fallen asleep next to Távas. He must've woken and snuck out. "I can't believe it. He ran. He left me." Aurora went over to her bright yellow couch and plopped down. "I don't understand. Why would he just go without a word?"

Ixy got up from the floor and sat beside her, taking her hand. "I'm sorry, sister, but what did you expect? He's too evil to cure, and he can't stay with you."

She sighed and shook her head. "But it doesn't make sense. I know he loves me. Otherwise, I couldn't be sitting here right now, as myself, unaffected by the plague."

Plus, here were the facts: she'd stuck her neck way, way out for him with her brethren. She'd fought for his life, knowing that it hadn't just made her look a fool, but that it made her doubt her own sanity. Loving him required her to completely accept him. *To have complete faith in him, too.* She would never do anything like that for just anyone. He was special.

"Would it be completely irrational to hold out hope he'll come back?" Aurora asked, imagining Távas the night he'd showed up to her hotel room in his sexy suit with red roses in hand. It was the night she'd learned that he had a big, big heart underneath it all. His rudeness had been an effort to prevent her from feeling attracted to him. He wanted to keep her at a distance because he'd needed to stay good and be there for Louie, which meant denying himself the woman he'd pined for, for over two thousand years.

A man willing to do that wasn't hopeless.

"I do not know, sister," said Ixy. "But…"

"But what?"

Ixy sighed. "The part of me that knows better wants you to let go and seek happiness elsewhere, because if anyone deserves it, it's you. The other part of me knows that if I were in your shoes, and he were Antonio, I would never give up. Not ever."

Ixy had married an incubus-vampire, so she understood the whole odd-couple thing.

Aurora drew a breath. "I'm going to hold out hope. He's going to come back, and this will all work out somehow."

Ixy patted her hand. "Then let us hope he proves to be worthy of you, Aurora. Because at present, I cannot think of any man who is."

Ixy's cell phone rang, and she slid it from the

pocket inside her sunny dress. "Hello?" She looked at Aurora. "It's Acan, for you."

Aurora took the phone. "Hello?" She listened and then ended the call.

"What did he say?" Ixy asked.

"Távas took Louie." Dread filled her heart. Távas wasn't coming back. And the gods only knew what would become of that young man.

# CHAPTER EIGHTEEN

*One month later…*

Zac, God of Temptation, and the saddest mother-fucking deity on the planet, inhaled the cold ocean air and winced. It even hurt to breathe. Without Tula, nothing made sense. His soul was no longer in jeopardy of flipping—it would forever be bound to her—but what did it matter now?

"You're sure you want to see this?" Roen asked him, the large ocean freighter slowly rocking beneath their feet in the rough night waters.

"Yes." Zac gave a nod and zipped up his black parka. It was fucking freezing out here just off the coast of Alaska—at least, that was where he thought they were. The mermen had demanded he be blindfolded and remain indoors during the month-long voyage. No one was to know where Cimil was "buried," so to speak.

"Don't fucking care," Zac had said the moment they'd held out the blindfold. "I'd let you pluck out my eyes and cut off my manhood if it meant getting a front-row seat to Cimil's sinking."

"Do not tempt us, Zac, because we might take

you up on your offer," Roen had said. Zac knew those were empty words. The night Tula died, the merman had found them, albeit far too late. It was then that Zac told Roen what had really happened, how Cimil lied and Zac flipped. It all could've been avoided had Cimil simply told the truth. Or, at the very least, not intervened. But she had, and Tula had died because of it, along with many others. Even Minky was upset. Minky adored Tula.

*And now it's V-day.* No, not Valentine's. Vengeance day. Cimil had injured him in a way that could never be forgotten or forgiven. The worst part being that he simply couldn't understand why. What had she gained from such treachery?

*Guess we'll never know.*

"Dump her!" Roen commanded to three of his men who waited at the bow of the ship.

With a push, the black steel barrel tumbled over the side of the ship.

"Good fucking riddance to bad fucking rubbish," Zac muttered.

As the barrel sank, he felt lighter. Cimil would never hurt, manipulate, bully, or threaten him again. From this day forward, he would be free to live his existence knowing his choices were his own.

*Nobody puts Zaccy in the corner. And nobody hurts a soul like Tula's.* He glared down at the dark waters, feeling the five souls fade into nothing.

*Wait. Five?* His entire body stiffened. *No. It can't be.* He looked again, opening his senses. *Oh fuck.* Yes, there were five distinct lights fighting for their lives.

"Wait!" he screamed, rushing to Roen, who was speaking with his men. "Bring her back."

Roen gave him an unsympathetic look. "I advised you not to watch."

"No!" Zac grabbed Roen by the shoulders. "You don't understand. She wasn't lying. She really is pregnant."

At first Roen looked shocked, but his expression quickly turned to anger. "Away with you, Zac, God of Temptation. We will not fall for your tricks."

"This isn't a trick. There are five souls inside that drum. Five. I felt them all."

Roen shook his head. "One of Cimil's many scams, no doubt. You heard the Goddess of Fertility with your own ears—there are no babies."

"Well, I don't know how it's possible, but they are there. And they're half human—or whatever the hell Roberto is. They will die if you don't—"

Roen gave a nod, and his men descended upon Zac. "Take him to his cabin and sedate him. He can be freed once we return to port."

"That's in a month!" Zac kicked and screamed, but in his weakened state, he was no match for Roen's men. A broken heart meant a broken soul and broken everything. "Please," Zac begged as they hauled him off, "do not do this."

"It is already done. There is no way to retrieve your sister, so I suggest you accept her death, just as the eight widows have accepted the deaths of their husbands. Consider yourself lucky, Zac. Not only have we allowed you to live, but you will no longer be plagued by Cimil's evil."

They stuck him in the neck with something that instantly burned through his veins. His vision quickly blurred. "What was that?" he mumbled.

"Something to keep you quiet." The men tossed him in a small room with a steel door.

He lay there on the floor, holding up his hand, deliriously reaching for the four little lights on board that drum with Cimil. "No. Godsdammit no," he muttered. "It will be too late in a month."

Suddenly he saw two pairs of big blue eyes hovering over him. They were filled with so much love.

"Tula?" He strained, trying to focus his blurry vision. The eyes faded into nothing.

*A dream.* He began to sob. *I miss her so much.*

"Mr. Zac?" Something warm and wet slid over his cheek. He tried to open his eyes, but the drugs were powerful, beckoning him into a dream state. Hell, perhaps he was already asleep, because when he opened his eyes for a split second, he could've sworn he saw a fanged unicorn hovering inches from his face.

*With Tula's eyes and voice?* His immortal heartbeat skipped a beat, recalling that Minky had taken Tula's body and refused to give it back. *Oh no.*

# CHAPTER NINETEEN

"You ready for this?" Acan grabbed Forgetty's shoulder and gave it a squeeze.

No, she wasn't. Not in the least. But over the past thirty days, her hardwiring had compelled her to accept the painful truth: Távas was not coming back. Thus, she was at risk. At any moment he could cut the cord and sever their mate bond, therefore rejecting her and leaving her in the exact same position she'd sought to avoid at all costs: Flipped.

She gave her brother's hand a squeeze. "I'll survive."

"I suppose you will. After all, what choice is there when one lives forever?" He snorted.

She shrugged off his attempt to lighten the moment.

"But, sister," he warned, "you must let go. You must open yourself to the possibility of love. Otherwise, tonight is all for naught."

"I know. I do. But what if I don't meet someone else? What if Távas was it, and I'm left with nothing and flip?"

"It's a valid question, but if you flip, then you

do. We will figure it out. Together."

"You say that, but you'll forget—me, you, everything. It'll be a giant mess."

He chuckled softly. "If you think for one moment that I could ever forget Margarita or her daughter, Jessica—or even you—then you do not know the first thing about love. The soul never forgets."

Forgetty blinked back the tears threatening to flood her eyes, knowing in her heart it was true. Her followers never truly forgot her. Once a connection was made, time might dull it, but it never really went away. A person could smell something as simple as baby powder and be brought back to the loving embrace of their mother. An old song on the radio could propel that same person back to the exact moment in their lives they first heard it. For her, it was 1877 and the sound of a needle touching down on a tin sheet wrapped around a cylinder in her old living room.

*Sound. Recorded for all time.* "It is truly amazing," she'd said, poking at the thing Cimil had stolen from that Edison man. "To think that one can record their own voice to be heard a million years from now. Think of all the wisdom we can pass forward." Humans, for the first time ever, could use each generation as a stepping-stone. Not that the written word would not serve, but it did not convey emotion as easily or the truth in one's voice. As for learning to read books, that took time, education, and a thirst for enlightenment.

*Ah, but listening to a voice*—an elder, a grand-parent...*or even a goddess.* This was truly magical.

This memory gave her comfort as she contemplated letting go of Távas and opening herself to another. She would never truly lose him because his music, his sound, would forever remain in her heart.

"All right," she jerked her head, "bring on the men."

Acan smiled. "He'll be here. I promise."

"Who?"

"A man worthy of you."

Inspirational words, no doubt, but..."How do you know for sure?"

Acan shrugged. "Because I believe in gods, in us. And you, my dear sister, have the most generous heart I've ever known. The Universe will not turn her back on you, just as she didn't turn hers on me—a god who was lost inside a bottle since the invention of bottles. If there's hope for me, certainly there is for you." Acan walked toward the front doors of the Randy Unicorn, their flagship LA nightclub.

"Fuck." She pushed her hands through her long hair straightened to silky perfection for tonight's speed-dating event.

Forgetty groaned out a breath as the men lined up. She sat precariously in the center of the room at a small black table, one lonely glass of ice water in front of her—okay, okay. It was vodka. But who could blame her? Five hundred men were in wait, preparing to spend one minute convincing her that they might be worth her love. And for the next eight-plus hours, she would attempt the unthinkable: to find a male who could fill the void left by Távas.

If this didn't work, she didn't know what she'd do.

Acan walked up with the first man, Marcos— tall, dark, and handsome. *And a vampire. Who likes to complain about the stringent rules limiting which people he was allowed to eat.* She did not have time for this, she thought, as the guy went on and on for what felt like forever.

The buzzer finally sounded. *Thank gods.* "Next!"

A man with a rainbow wig, bright red nose, and sad face-paint sat down and honked his horn. *Squeak! Squeak!*

"Next!" she yelled over her shoulder, eliciting a whimper from her rejected date.

*You've got to be kidding me.* No man worthy of her love would dare to whimper.

She turned around and looked at the long line flowing outside the club.

*Oh, dear gods.* S&M bondage harnesses, more rainbow wigs, jugglers, a guy with a tiger and whip. Cimil had not been joking about using Vampire-freaks.com, clowndating, and fetlife.

*Fucking Cimil.* She laughed. Even at the bottom of the ocean she was up to her pranks. *Though, I have to admit, this is pretty funny.*

At least there were a few normal-looking guys; although, they appeared to be scared out of their minds due to the unusual crowd.

Hours and hours went by without so much as a tingle, let alone a spark. Rehearsed speeches, corny pickup lines, bad vampire jokes, and lots of clown honking. Some men were attractive; some were not. Some were nice, and some...well, they put Távas's jerk routine to shame, though they weren't acting. She sat motionless through the parade of suitors who didn't hold a match to the evil king who embodied something she found genuinely attractive: his strength. Távas represented the fight within us all. Because life could be downright ugly.

Some of us fought to live another day.

Some of us lived to fight another day.

Either way it was a fight.

And while she could never condone Távas's actions, or the way he'd chosen to fight, she understood why he'd done it. He'd wanted to save his family. Then, hoping to be worthy of her love, he fought to be more. More powerful, in control, worthy of admiration.

It hadn't worked out.

*Or had it?* She admired his strength, didn't she? On the down side, Ixy couldn't cure him. Just why was that, exactly?

Perhaps he really was too powerful. But now that she thought about it, the likelier answer was that the Universe had her own plan. She did, after all, demand that every beauty have a flaw, every life have a death, and every day have a night.

*Jesus, that's it.* It had never occurred to her until now that the Universe had chosen Távas, too. To be evil. It was the reason that Ixy, Antonio, and three incubi could not cure him. He couldn't be cured because he wasn't meant to be. He was no different than any of the gods chosen to play a role.

So then what? If she was right, then where did that leave her and Távas? If his purpose was to be darkness, where the hell did that leave her broken heart?

It was an impossible puzzle.

She sighed.

"Forgetty? Your final date is here," said Acan. "Do you want to see him?"

It was now six in the morning.

"Why not?" She gave a shallow nod.

She heard Acan's heavy footsteps fade off to the door. "Come in."

"How is she?" said a deep, familiar voice.

"See for yourself, king," said Acan.

*King?* Forgetty pivoted in her seat. Across the room stood the most gorgeous man she'd ever seen. He was seven feet of wicked male in a suit that contoured his deadly strength and muscles. His short, dirty blond hair was a fucking mess, and his dark beard looked like something the devil himself might wear.

*Gods fucking dammit, he's sexy.* Lucifer had nothing on him.

"Aurora," Távas said, without emotion.

She rose on her shaking knees, unable to breathe right. "Távas, what are you doing here? And where is your Maaskab outfit?" She could see ribbons of black swirling through his aura, meaning he was still as wicked as ever.

"It is a very long story, one I will explain after I've said what I've come to say."

"And Louie? Is he all right?"

"He is fine, actually. Better than fine."

"That's good." *Unexpected, but good.*

"Aurora," he took her hand, clasping it between his own, "I've spent the last month searching for answers, wondering how to make sense of you, of me, of any of this, only to come up with very few answers—none of which have changed the fundamentals of our perplexing situation. So I'm here to ask you one question."

"Y-yes?"

"Can you love a wicked man who's completely unredeemable?"

Her soul swelled. "Is he part of the Universe's master plan, and anything he does is ultimately for the greater good of humanity?"

He shook his head. "I have no fucking clue."

In all honesty, neither did she. All she knew was that they were opposite sides of the coin and they both had a purpose.

He continued, "But if you will forever be a goddess and I cannot see my life without you, nor can I be changed, then that only leaves us with one option: to be together as we are. For better or worse. Okay, lots of worse, in my case, but you get the picture."

As she stared into his blue eyes flecked with lavender, he undid her in the most soul-felt, carnal, wicked of ways, reducing her to the most primitive form possible.

*I need him. I do. But how can we make this work?* Then it hit her smack-dab in the middle of the forehead.

The Universe had chosen her for a role very few could endure. Her suffering came with the job, but she had figured out how to get on.

*I can figure this out, too.* Though, it meant accepting what was, not what she hoped or thought it should be. In her mind, she saw herself with Távas only if he was cured. But perhaps there was another way?

*Hell, if someone could love Cimil—okay, horrible example since that didn't end well because she messed it up.* Still, Roberto never cared that Cimil had an evil streak. In fact, he sort of dug it. *And I have to admit, there is a certain attraction to being mated to a bad boy.* Bad boys were sexy.

Aurora gave Távas a coy smile. "What are gods without monsters, and monsters without gods?"

Távas grinned. "Bored. They would be utterly

bored."

"Exactly." She smiled back at him.

Music exploded over the nightclub's speakers, and the dance floor lit up in a hundred multicolored lights.

She knew the song. "You're in Love with a Psycho" by Kasabian. She'd spun it at the last three tours in her closing mash-up.

"Are you in love with a psycho?" Távas asked.

"No. You are. Because I'm absolutely crazy about you."

They kissed and fireworks exploded.

❧ ❧

Acan wrapped his arm around Margarita. He knew tonight was a risk, but his dear, sweet Forgetty had given him so much over the years—friendship, unconditional love, bail money—how could he not go the extra mile for her and ensure the evil king came to present his case? One thing Acan had learned from his long existence, filled with countless mistakes, was that sometimes you just had to have faith. *When one embarks on a long journey, one does not see the entire road. You simply take one step at a time, trusting it will eventually lead to your destination.* He hoped it would be the same for Aurora and Távas because clearly the two loved each other, even if they did not know how it would work out.

"They look really happy." Margarita smiled at

the couple making out in the middle of the dance floor.

Acan sighed. "They do."

"I just wonder if the indoor fireworks were a good choice."

He too noted the walls on fire. "Just give them another minute before dialing 911. She deserves it."

Margarita nodded. "Not the first nightclub you've burnt to the ground."

"Won't be the last."

"It's part of your charm," she offered.

Acan hugged her. "Gods, I love that you get me, woman."

"And I love that you love that I get you."

They faced each other and began making out.

# CHAPTER TWENTY

"All right, keep your eyes closed." Távas held his hands over Aurora's eyes as he unlocked the door to some mysterious building in downtown LA.

"They're closed, but you're sure I'm not going to open my eyes to some horrible scene of human sacrifice."

"No." He chuckled. "My days of sacrificing humans have long past. Along with warring with the gods and your army."

They continued walking, she with her hands extended. In all honesty, she was enjoying this. Távas was all clean and smelled really nice. What wasn't to love?

"Okay. So no more human sacrifices, no more war with us—what does that leave a monster like you to do with his time?" she asked.

He dropped his hands. "Open your eyes."

Slowly, she cracked one lid. It was a large restaurant with bright yellow walls and cartoon paintings of happy chickens flying old single-prop planes.

"I've gone into the chicken-murdering business!" he said proudly.

"Huh?"

"Wings. It's a chicken wings restaurant. I've purchased ten of them across the country. Louie is going to help me expand to fifty more sites."

Her mouth fell open. "I, uh…I, uh…but wait? So…I…" She scratched the side of her head. "You're the Maaskab king and now you own chicken wings restaurants?"

"We serve one hundred varieties of beer, too."

"But why? How?" This was beyond bizarre.

"After I left your apartment, Louie and I went to my home in Malibu."

"You have a house in Malibu?"

"Built it last year. Right on the water. And it blocks the view of ten other houses." He grinned proudly. "It's quite evil, if I do say so myself."

She cocked a brow.

"Anyway, Louie and I had a long talk about our place in the world and what to do next if we were unchangeable. Neither of us had answers, but we did get hungry, so I ordered wings—they still taste good even if I can't fully enjoy their sinfulness due to my evilness. But as he and I sat there licking our fingers and enjoying deep-fried, unhealthy food, Louie said something that clicked with me."

"What?"

"He said, 'It's a shame that you have to be a Maaskab, Dad. I mean, think of all the interesting ways there are to be evil in this day and age.'"

Aurora blinked. "And that led you to buying this place?"

"Better. I realized that while my powers and history are certainly ancient, Louie was right. There are plenty of evil, horrible, successful people out in the world today. I don't need to run around all sticky and with thumb jewelry. The days of the Mayans and the Maaskab are over, and it's time for me to find a new place in the new world."

"So that's it? Just like that?"

"Yeah. I cleaned myself up, stopped eating black jade, and the next day Louie and I began making plans. Wings and beer to start, all very unhealthy. I'm also looking into funding some very violent video game companies. Eventually, once I get bored of that, then I think I'll get into politics."

"Seems like a logical place for someone who wants to mess up the world," Aurora muttered, her mind trying to absorb all this.

"Does it please you?" he asked.

She blinked up at him. "Well, yeah. I mean, it's really quite brilliant."

"I have to admit, I don't think this would be possible without you, Aurora. Through our bond, you've given me just enough control over my sadistic nature to find nonviolent outlets for my powers."

She bobbed her head, still processing. In a really, really weird way, he'd just given her everything she'd hoped for. "Thank you, Távas."

"For what?"

"Thank you for doing this—for finding another

way."

"Well," his blue eyes flashed to lavender for a brief moment, "I will still need help." He stepped closer, letting her feel the heat of his ridiculously strong body, flooding her mind with memories of his soft lips.

"With what?"

"I have other cravings, and they are all quite sinister." He slid his warm hand to the back of her neck, lust twinkling in his eyes.

"Oh, so…you mean you're going to need lots of sex?"

He nodded. "Dirty sex. The dirtiest."

*Dirty, huh?* She doubted he could come up with anything that would shock her. In her years, she'd seen everything. Humans could get quite creative when it came to kink.

Nevertheless, the challenge aroused her.

She swallowed down the lump in her throat, feeling every inch of her body tingle. "We-well, I don't break easily, and I'm fairly sure there isn't much that would be off the table."

He flashed a charming, sadistic grin. "I am so, so glad you said that."

&c~&

"Are you sure about this?" Aurora said from the bedroom of her apartment while Távas waited in the other room. "I feel kind of silly."

"You said you were game for anything!" he yelled.

She scratched her naked arm. *I suppose I did, but this is a little weird. And itchy!* On the other hand, if this did it for him and it kept his evil side in check, who was she to argue?

"Okay," she said in a gruff, throaty monster voice, "I'm coming for you, you naughty man."

She popped the big chef's knife between her teeth and marched into the living room, where Távas sat duct taped to one of her dining room chairs.

His beautiful eyes lit up with sexual hunger.

"You want some of this?" She spun in a circle, allowing him to drink in her nearly naked body covered in a paste made of fake blood and charcoal. To complete her outfit, she had on a necklace made of plastic thumbs and a suede thong. She'd drawn the line at using anything made of real human body parts. *'Cause ick!*

"Yes, I do. I want all of it," he said, his voice low and saturated with lust.

"Ah, then you have to tell me how bad you've been."

"Why don't you remove this duct tape and I can show you?"

Honestly, the tape had been her idea. She kept thinking about how sexy Távas had looked the night she'd flipped and tied him up.

"Sorry. If you want to be free, you have to pay

the evil priestess." She stood directly in front of him with her ass turned toward his face.

He made a deep groan as she lowered herself into his lap, sliding her ass over the thick bulge in his groin. Her eyes rolled to the back of her head. He felt so good, so hard. She didn't know how long she'd be able to keep up this charade.

*Not long. I've waited forever for this moment.* She turned and got to her knees.

"Oh no. You can't," he protested. "Our first time together can't be that."

He thought she was going to suck him off? Not a chance. She wanted their bodies joined and moving together in perfect, wicked, sinful harmony.

*Still, I should tease him a little.*

She took her knife and started slicing up one pant leg. "Let's see what our bad human has hidden under here." She stopped cutting just inches from his hard cock, which was thrusting against the soft black fabric of his pants. She then tore the fabric the rest of the way with her bare hands.

"Oh my. Now that *is* wicked." Wicked sexy. His velvety cock was long and thick and veined to a hard perfection.

She licked her lips and dipped her head, unable to resist testing the softness with her mouth. She kissed the top of his crown, eliciting his deep groan.

Távas threw back his head and clawed his fingertips into the arm of the chair.

Now that he was back to his old self, more or

less, she knew he could break free at any point. He was stronger than most of the gods, and when his physical strength didn't cut it, he had other tricks up his sleeve.

Feeling her core flutter and her entire body light up with arousal, she took him in, attempting to encase him in the warmth of her mouth.

"Oh, goddess. You need to stop that or I will cu—"

She pulled back her head and then slid her mouth down on him again until he hit her deep in the throat.

He called out in ecstasy. "Okay. You...win..." He groaned his words.

She stroked him again with her mouth, savoring the salty heat of him. But now, it was her own need driving her actions. She needed him inside her, coming hard.

She stood, removed her suede bottoms, and turned around, planting herself in his lap, placing his hard shaft between her soft aching folds. Slowly, she rocked herself against his cock, spreading her wetness up and down the hard length of him. She moaned with each inch, feeling her c-spot throb with need.

"Please, more," he begged.

"Yes, that's what I want to hear; beg me." This hadn't been part of their agreed-upon role-playing, but dammit if it did fit.

"Please put me inside you," he asked, nearly

demanding.

She rocked her hips and used her hand to hold his erection firmly against the slick valley between her legs. "Say it again. Like you mean it, my evil king."

Suddenly, he broke free of the tape and wrapped his strong arms around her waist, pushing her forward, down onto the carpet on all fours.

"Please," he said, and then thrust into her from behind, stealing her breath, the warmth of his strong chest covering her back.

She gasped with pleasure, feeling him stretch and fill her.

"You're so fucking warm, so fucking tight." He pulled out and slammed into her again.

She moaned, her hands clawing into the rug. "You're my first."

He stopped moving. "What?"

*Oh gods. How embarrassing.* "I thought you knew—all that talk about angry sex you gave me."

He pulled out and lifted himself away. She twisted and sat to face him. "What's the matter? Why did you stop?"

He kneeled in front of her, taking her hand and kissing the top, allowing his lips to linger for a long moment. "I was egging you on, Aurora. But had I known this was your first time…"

"What? I'm enjoying it." In fact, she was a little peeved that he'd stopped.

"We have an eternity for dirty sex, duct tape,

and shredding our clothes. But there is only one first time, and you deserve to be bedded properly." He dropped her hand and ran his through his thick dirty blond hair. "I should've known."

"No. It's okay. Really. I don't need flowers and candles. I've spent my entire life being forgotten— no chocolates, no birthday cards, no—"

"I didn't think gods had birthdays."

"We don't, but we pretend. The point is, I've been invisible for seventy thousand years and the fact that you see me, that you love me and don't care that I'm not perfect or not all-knowing and that I have no experience in bed," she drew a breath, "I can't think of a better memory than that for my first time." She shrugged. "Plus, you kinda already put it in me, so it's a moot point. First time…over!" She threw up her hands. "Can I come now?"

He smiled, but it was unlike any smile she'd ever seen on a man. It came from the inside and radiated out.

"You take my breath away, Távas. You're so beautiful. I truly mean that."

"I haven't been able to forget you since we first met two thousand years ago. I don't know how it's possible to love someone and not know them, but I did. Love at first sight. Marry me, Aurora. Because I won't ever love another. And I want to do evil sexy things to you."

She didn't think it possible, but she could swear she felt all of the tiny cracks in her soul filling up.

"You're my mate. You're part of me now. And yes, I will marry you."

"Good." He got to his feet and took her hand, jerking her up.

"What are you—"

He quickly threw her over his shoulder, heading off in the direction of her bedroom. "Role-playing is over. It's time for reality." He threw her onto the bed and then crawled toward her until his naked muscled body hovered over her.

"What now?" She panted her words, completely breathless.

"I worship at your altar for the next four hours."

"And then?"

"And then we figure it out one day at a time. But rest assured, my goddess, you will never ever be forgotten or neglected again. I pledge my wicked heart to that."

## TO BE CONTINUED

# AUTHOR'S NOTE

Want more chaotic gods? Me too! COLEL, the Goddess of Bees, is next in line. Check her page for updates:

www.mimijean.net/colel.html

OR...EVEN EASIER! Sign up for new release alerts and random weird crap in my monthly newsletters:

https://goo.gl/9NZiqR

Newsletter not weird enough for ya? Then there's my awesome fan group. (Yeah, it's exactly like you imagine.) facebook.com/groups/MimiJeansJunkies

As for SWAG, you know what to do. Send an email to mimi@mimijean.net with your full name and shipping address (international okay), and I will send you something awesome from my monthly mail out. Don't FORGETTY (har, har) to mention if you took your valuable time to show the book-love and write a review! I will surely thank you and possibly send a coveted fridge magnet. (First-come basis—I do run out.)

What sort of crazy-ass songs fueled this crazy-ass book? Find out here...

open.spotify.com/user/mimijeanpamfiloff/playlist/6dV9w56DrZXRunlphqXeaG?si=RvWkjnpeTx-az5IQiAEQVw

Alrighty, my lovely goddesses! I hope you enjoyed the adventure. I'm back to work, writing *SKINNY PANTS*. (Yes, I know. LOL! It's only like three years overdue!)

**With Love,**
Mimi, Author of 30 Books and Counting

# ACKNOWLEDGMENTS

I can't forget Su, Latoya, Pauline, Paul, Dali, Kylie, and Ally… I can't remember what I wanted to say. Oh! Thank you for being a part of book #30!

To my guys, I always think of you when I'm holed up in my office, trying to finish a book. Love you.

*Mimi*

# Character Definitions – The Gods

Although every culture around the world has their own names and beliefs related to beings of worship, there are actually only fourteen gods. And since the gods are able to access the human world only through the portals called cenotes, located in the Yucatán, the Mayans were big fans.

Another fun fact: The gods often refer to each other as brother and sister, but the truth is they are just another species of the Creator and completely unrelated.

**Acan**—God of Wine and Intoxication, and God of Decapitation. Also known as Belch, Acan has been drunk for many millennia. He generally wears only tighty whities, but since he's the life of the party, he's been known to mix it up and go naked, too. Whatever works. He is now mated to the lovely Margarita.

**Ah-Ciliz**—God of Solar Eclipses: Called A.C. by his brethren, Ah-Ciliz is generally thought of as a giant buzz kill because of his dark attitude.

**Akna**—Goddess of Fertility: She is so powerful, it is said she can make inanimate objects fornicate and that anyone who gets in the same room as her ends up pregnant. She is often seen hanging out with her brother Acan at parties, when not hiding in a cave.

**Backlum Chaam**—God of Male Virility: He was once a slave to the Maaskab and played a key role in discovering that black jade can be used to procreate with humans.

**Camaxtli**—Goddess of the Hunt: Also once known as Fate until she was discovered to be a fake and had her powers stripped away by the Universe. She's now referred to as "Fake."

**Colel Cab**—Mistress of Bees: Though she has many, many powers, "Bees" is most known for the live beehive hat on her head. She has never had a boyfriend or lover because her bees get too jealous.

**Goddess of Forgetfulness**—She has no official name that is known of and has the power to make anyone forget anything. She spends her evenings DJing because she finds the anonymity of dance clubs to be comforting. Her partner in crime is Acan, the God of Wine.

**Ixtab**—Goddess of Happiness (ex-Goddess of Suicide): Ixtab's once morbid frock used to make children scream. But since finding her soul mate, she's now the epitome of all things happy.

**K'ak (Pronounced "cock")**—The history books remember him as K'ak Tiliw Chan Yopaat, ruler of Copán in the 700s AD. King K'ak is one of Cimil's favorite brothers. We're not really sure what he does, but he can throw bolts of lightning, wears a giant silver and jade headdress with intertwining serpents, and has long black and silver hair.

**Kinich Ahau**—ex-God of the Sun: Known by many other names, depending on the culture, Kinich likes to go by Nick these days. He's also now a vampire—something he's actually not so bummed about. He is mated to the love of his life, Penelope, the Ruler of the House of Gods.

**Máax**—Once known as the God of Truth, Máax was banished for repeatedly violating the ban on time travel. However, since helping to save the world from the big "over," he is now known as the God of Time Travel. Also turns out he was the God of Love, but no one figured that out until his mate, Ashli, inherited his power. Ashli is now the fourteenth deity, taking the place of Camaxtli, the Fake.

**Votan**—God of Death and War: Also known as Odin, Wotan, Wodan, God of Drums (he has no idea how the hell he got that title; he hates drums), and Lord of Multiplication (okay, he is pretty darn good at math so that one makes sense). These days, Votan goes by Guy Santiago (it's a long story—read *ACCIDENTALLY IN LOVE WITH...A GOD?*), but despite his deadly tendencies, he's all heart.

**Yum Cimil**—Goddess of the Underworld: Also known as Ah-Puch by the Mayans, Mictlantecuhtli (try saying that one ten times) by the Aztec, Grim Reaper by the Europeans, Hades by the Greeks…you get the picture! Despite what people say, Cimil is actually a female, adores a good bargain (especially garage sales) and the color pink, and she hates clowns. She's also bat-shit crazy, has an invisible pet unicorn named Minky, and is married to Roberto, the king of all vampires.

**Zac Cimi**—Once thought to be the God of Love, we now know differently. Zac is the God of Temptation, and his tempting ways have landed him in very hot water. Because no matter how temptingly hot your brother's mate might be, trying to steal her is wrong. He is currently serving time for his crime in Los Angeles with Cimil, running the Immortal Matchmakers agency. He is now madly in love with his assistant, Tula.

# Character Definitions – Not the Gods

**Andrus:** Ex-Demilord (vampire who's been given the gods' light), now just a demigod after his maker, the vampire queen, died. He is now happily mated to Sadie, a half-succubus who spends her days feeding off of her delicious new hubby and going to casting calls in LA.

**Ashli:** Ashli actually belongs over in the GODS section, but since she was born human, we'll keep her here. Ashli is mate to Máax, God of Time Travel. Unbeknownst to him, he was also the God of Love. Ashli inherited his power after they started falling in love. Maybe the Universe thought a woman should have this power?

**Brutus:** One of the gods' elite Uchben warriors. He doesn't speak much, but that's because he and his team are telepathic. They are also immortal (a gift from the gods) and next in line to be Uchben chiefs.

**Charlotte:** Sadie's golf-loving half-sister and the intended mate to Andrus Grey. Only, Andrus, being the rebel that he is, decided he could pick his own damned woman, Sadie. Charlotte is now happily mated to Tommaso, Andrus's BBF. They're one big happy family! Oh, and her daddy is an incubus.

**Helena Strauss:** Once human, Helena is now a vampire and married to Niccolo DiConti. She has a half-vampire daughter, Matty, who is destined to marry Andrus's son, according to Cimil.

**Margarita Seville:** Once a member of the Amish community, Margarita now lives in LA, following her calling to make the world a healthier place. She owns a successful gym and has a teenage daughter, Jessica, who's hell-bent on making her life miserable. She is mate to Acan, God of Wine.

**Matty:** The infant daughter of Helena and Niccolo, destined to marry Andrus's son.

**Niccolo DiConti:** General of the Vampire Army. Now that the vampire queen is dead, the army remains loyal to him. He shares power with his wife, Helena Strauss, and has a half-vampire daughter, Matty.

**Reyna:** The dead vampire queen.

**Roberto (Narmer):** Originally an Egyptian pharaoh, Narmer was one of the six Ancient Ones—the very first vampires. He eventually changed his name to Roberto and moved to Spain—something to do with one of Cimil's little schemes. He now spends his days lovingly undoing Cimil's treachery, being a stay-at-home dad, and taking her unicorn Minky for a ride.

**Sadie:** Charlotte's half sister and mated to Andrus Grey, Sadie is an aspiring actress who discovered she's also half incubus.

**Távas:** Hero of this book, so I can't spoil who he truly is. But it's a doozy!

**Tommaso:** Once a soldier of the gods, called Uchben, Tommaso's mind was poisoned with black jade. He tried to kill Emma, Votan's mate, but redeemed himself by turning into a spy for the gods. He is now mated to Charlotte.

**Tula:** The incorruptible administrative assistant at Immortal Matchmakers, Inc.

# COMING 2018!
# SKINNY PANTS
## BOOK 4, THE HAPPY PANTS SERIES

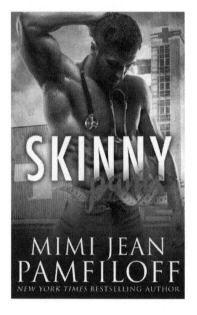

He's the doctor of her dreams.

She's got room to lose.

But this plump ER nurse will have to face facts:

A solid relationship begins when you're ready to take it all off.

www.mimijean.net/skinny-pants.html

# DIGGING A HOLE

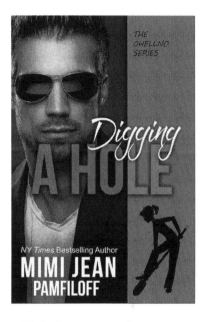

**He's the meanest boss ever.**
**She's the sweet shy intern.**
**They're about to wreck each other crazy.**

My name is Sydney Lucas. I am smart, deathly shy, and one hundred percent determined to make my own way in the world. Which is why I jumped at the chance to intern for Mr. Nick Brooks despite his reputation. After ten failed interviews at other companies, he was the only one offering. Plus, everyone says he knows his stuff, and surely a man as stunningly handsome as him can't be "the devil incarnate," right? Wrong.

Oh…that man. That freakin' man has got to go! I've been on the job one week, and he's insulted my mother, wardrobe shamed me, and managed to make me cry. Twice. Underneath that stone-cold, beautiful face is the evilest human being ever.

But I'm not going to quit. Oh no. For once in my life, I've got to make a stand. Only, every time I open my mouth, I can't quite seem to muster the courage. Perhaps my revenge needs to come in another form: destroying him quietly.

Because I've got a secret. I'm not really just an intern, and Sydney Lucas isn't my real name.

### FOR EXTRAS, BUY LINKS, and MORE, GO TO:

www.mimijean.net/diggingahole.html

# CHECK

### Get ready for BOOK THREE of
### Mr. Rook's Island!

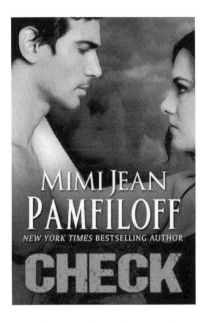

(You won't guess the ending, unless you're
completely devious like Mimi.)

For Excerpts, Buy Links, and More:
www.mimijean.net/check.html

# ABOUT THE AUTHOR

MIMI JEAN PAMFILOFF is a *New York Times* bestselling romance author who's sold over one million books around the world. Although she obtained her MBA and worked for more than fifteen years in the corporate world, she believes that it's never too late to come out of the romance closet and follow your dream. Mimi lives with her Latin lover hubby, two pirates-in-training (their boys), and the rat terrier duo, Snowflake and Mini Me, in Arizona. She hopes to make you laugh when you need it most and continues to pray daily that leather pants will make a big comeback for men.

Sign up for Mimi's mailing list for giveaways and new release news!

*STALK MIMI:*
www.mimijean.net
twitter.com/MimiJeanRomance
pinterest.com/mimijeanromance
instagram.com/mimijeanpamfiloff
facebook.com/MimiJeanPamfiloff

Printed in Germany
by Amazon Distribution
GmbH, Leipzig